Emily Harvale lives in
– although she would prefer to live in the French Alps ... or Canada ... or anywhere that has several months of snow. Emily loves snow almost as much as she loves Christmas. Having worked in the City (London) for several years, Emily returned to her home town of Hastings where she spends her days writing ... and wondering if it will ever snow. You can contact her via her website, Facebook or Instagram.

There is also a Facebook group where fans can chat with Emily about her books, her writing day and life in general. Details can be found on Emily's website.

Author contacts:
www.emilyharvale.com
www.twitter.com/emilyharvale
www.facebook.com/emilyharvalewriter
www.instagram.com/emilyharvale

***

Scan the code above to see all Emily's books on Amazon

Also by this author

The Golf Widows' Club
Sailing Solo
Carole Singer's Christmas
Christmas Wishes
A Slippery Slope
The Perfect Christmas Plan
Be Mine
It Takes Two
Bells and Bows on Mistletoe Row

Lizzie Marshall series:
Highland Fling – book 1
Lizzie Marshall's Wedding – book 2

Goldebury Bay series:
Ninety Days of Summer – book 1
Ninety Steps to Summerhill – book 2
Ninety Days to Christmas – book 3

Hideaway Down series:
A Christmas Hideaway – book 1
Catch A Falling Star – book 2
Walking on Sunshine – book 3
Dancing in the Rain – book 4

Hall's Cross series
Deck the Halls – book 1
The Starlight Ball – book 2

Michaelmas Bay series
Christmas Secrets in Snowflake Cove – book 1
Blame it on the Moonlight – book 2

Lily Pond Lane series
The Cottage on Lily Pond Lane – four-part serial
Part One – New beginnings
Part Two – Summer secrets
Part Three – Autumn leaves

ISBN 978-1-909917-89-7

Published by Crescent Gate Publishing

Print edition published worldwide 2023
E-edition published worldwide 2023

Cover design by JR and Emily Harvale

Emily Harvale

A Date
at the end of
The Pier

CRESCENT GATE PUBLISHING

Acknowledgements

My grateful thanks go to the following:

My webmaster, David Cleworth who does so much more than website stuff.
My cover design team, JR.
Luke Brabants. Luke is a talented artist and can be found at: www.lukebrabants.com
My wonderful friends for their friendship and love. You know I love you all.
All the fabulous members of my Readers' Club. You help and support me in so many ways and I am truly grateful for your ongoing friendship. I wouldn't be where I am today without you.
My Twitter and Facebook friends, and fans of my Facebook author page. It's great to chat with you. You help to keep me (relatively) sane!

To view a map of Norman Landing visit

the maps page on my website

www.emilyharvale.com

To Mum and Dad,
always loved, never forgotten.
Still miss you every day.

One

'I'll be leaving in thirty minutes. An hour at the latest.'

'Yeah right,' my sister Katie says.

Nan, our gran, is also on the video call. Her name is Nancy, but everybody calls her Nan. 'If Katie and I had a pound for every time you told us you'd be leaving work at a reasonable hour,' she says, 'we'd both be very rich women.'

They're standing in my kitchen and, while Nan takes two glasses from the cupboard and places them on the worktop, Katie helps herself to a bottle of wine from my cooler.

'And if you two stopped drinking my wine, so would I.'

They grin at one another like mischievous children and then at me. I don't mind at all and Katie and Nan know that. Besides, Nan is currently staying at my house, so it's as much her home as mine, for

1

a few more days, at least.

Nan and her partner, Donald have recently bought a bungalow about five minutes' walk away from my house. They've already completed the purchase but they're having some work done and won't be moving in until that's finished. Donald had been staying with his daughter, who also lives nearby, but she's been causing a lot of upset over the last few months so I agreed he should come and join Nan at mine. He was there most days in any case, so it doesn't make that much difference.

Although I will admit, there have been times when I wished the walls in the house were thicker, or preferably, completely soundproofed. There's something slightly disconcerting about knowing that your gran and her partner, who are both in their eighties, are enjoying a much more active sex life than you are at almost thirty-one.

'If you stopped buying such good wine,' Katie says, still grinning, 'we'd stop drinking it.'

'Oh I see. It's my fault.'

'Obviously,' says Katie, as she pulls the cork from the bottle and tosses the bottle opener to one side.

'Oi! Wash that and put it back in the drawer, please.'

I don't know how many times I must tell

her stuff like that. Sometimes it amazes me that she's five years older than me.

She winks. 'I'll do it when I wash the glasses, grumpy.'

'So what time will you be back, sweetheart?' Nan asks.

This is the second call within the last ninety minutes, to check when I'm leaving work, so I'm tempted to say that if they stopped calling me, I'd get my work done faster, but I'm fairly certain what they'd say to that.

'By 7 p.m. or thereabouts.'

Katie frowns. 'Can't you get away any earlier?'

'That's cutting it fine,' Nan adds.

They're clearly not convinced I'll be home in time to meet up with them together with Donald, and Katie's partner, Aaron (who also happens to be my next-door neighbour) and make it to Alberto's Italian restaurant by 7.30 this evening.

I don't know what the big deal is. Okay, so I spend most of my life working, and I've been working even more hours recently. What can I say? I work for a major, computer software company, one of the top companies in the UK, and our state-of-the-art accounting software is increasingly in demand. Our clients are mainly blue-chip companies, and international and multinational corporations (not many smaller businesses can afford even our 'starter packages') and, as such, they expect to receive twenty-four-hour support, and that's what they get. We go above and beyond to keep our clients around the globe, happy. That's one of the reasons we're so busy.

But Katie and Nan both know I'm never late. If I agree to be somewhere at a certain time, I'm there on the dot. Or I'm early. But I'm never, ever late. Not that it really matters tonight if I am. They can all go on ahead without me and I can meet them there. I'll still be at the table on time.

'I promise I'll be home soon,' I reassure them. 'But even if I'm not, I can simply meet you at Alberto's. In any case, I can stake my life on the fact that, whatever happens, I'll be there before Tori and Mack, and as this evening is to celebrate Tori officially reopening Seascape Café tomorrow, surely that's what's important?'

'Fine,' says Katie, grudgingly. She can't really argue with that. Tori is often late.

'And I can always go straight to the restaurant. I don't need to go home and change.'

As they both tell me what they think about that, in no uncertain terms, the phone on my desk rings, so I quickly say, 'goodbye,' wave at them, and end the call.

'There's trouble in the trenches, Em.' It's Ben Affleck.

Unfortunately, not *the* Ben Affleck, the gorgeous actor – although my Ben does bear an uncanny resemblance and could easily pass as a close, younger relative. Sadly though, my Ben is not related to that Ben in any way, shape, or form.

And when I say, 'my Ben' what I mean is, he works with me in the 'new client team', not that he's actually mine. Which is also sad, because I've had a bit of a crush on him for several years. Since the day he joined the company, soon after me, in fact.

Ben is head of sales. I'm head of installation and training. Basically, Ben's team sells the product to the new client, and I ensure that my team handles the installation smoothly, and that the client's staff receive training on how the software works on a day-to-day basis. That means me and my team must go to the client's offices, wherever in the world that might be, so we're on hand to supervise the installation and to sort things out if anything goes wrong during the first few weeks. After that, the support teams take over and they are on-call via phone or video call, twenty-four-seven. But during those first few weeks, the responsibility for the smooth running of the product remains with Ben and his team and me and mine.

Ben and I get on well and we rarely disagree about what needs to be done to resolve any issues. We bounce ideas and solutions off one another and there's never been any sort of one-upmanship by either of us.

Sometimes, we even flirt with one another, although I hate to admit this because I am thirty-one in a matter of months, but I'm still a little shy when I'm attracted to someone. And I'm definitely attracted to Ben.

We did actually kiss once. Very briefly. But that was just over five years ago, at someone's birthday drinks one evening after work. I can't recall whose birthday it was, or anything much about that night because we'd all had a lot to drink, except that it was a Monday, and the person was leaving the following day. So it was really a birthday slash leaving do. But that Monday night was the night my mum died, so other than the brief kiss with Ben, Mum's death is all I remember about that day, or week, or month.

Mum was only fifty-eight and had never been seriously unwell. There wasn't even a hint that anything was wrong with her health. The cardiac arrest was completely unexpected and we have no idea what caused it, but it's known as Sudden Adult Death

Syndrome, and it's not as rare as you might think.

My boss insisted I took two weeks of compassionate leave at the time, and when I returned to work, other than Ben expressing his sincere condolences and telling me to let him know if there was anything he could do, he kept his distance and neither of us mentioned that kiss. And we haven't, to this day.

Not long after, Ben got a girlfriend, so whether or not there might have been anything between us romantically, I'll never know. Since then, we've just been work colleagues really.

I did invite him to my moving in party when I bought my house last July, and to my thirtieth birthday bash last October, but both dates clashed with prior engagements, so he was unable to come to either one. I hadn't really felt much like having any parties after Mum died, so those two last year were the first for a long time.

Mum loved a party, but we didn't have much money after Dad left when I was five and Katie was ten, so parties were a rare occasion. Nan sold her home and moved in with us to help out, but despite a serious lack of funds at times, we were happy. Mum and Nan always made birthday cakes for me and Katie, and we would always get a present, either something homemade or something 'preloved' as Nan and Mum called it. That meant something purchased from a local, charity shop. And fish and chips were a special treat.

Mum also loved to dance, and I can still see her and Nan, and me and Katie bopping around the living room. Mum had a beautiful smile, a melodious laugh like the trill of a happy bird, and a soft voice as warm as her hugs. The scent of lavender reminds me of her, and of her homemade lavender soap, and I miss her so much that my heart still breaks when I think of her.

Now, my heart flutters just a teensy-weensy bit at the sound of Ben's voice. Again, it's much like the 'other' Ben's, only without the American accent.

And then my heart skips a beat, but not in a good way, as his words register in my brain.

'What kind of trouble, Ben?'

'DEFCON 3.'

Ben sometimes says things one wouldn't expect a thirty-five-year-old man to say, and he watches far too many action movies and thrillers for his own good. I'm not sure why he chose to work for a computer software company, and not the military, or the UK government, but I trust his judgement implicitly. And his commitment to after sales service is second to none.

'What? You have got to be kidding me,' I say.

'Nope. It's gonna be a late one.'

I close my eyes for a second and a sigh escapes me. 'Why did it have to be tonight?'

'Is there a problem?'

'Yeah. I'm supposed to be at a restaurant at 7.30 and I've just this minute confirmed I won't be late, no matter what.'

'You're never late, Em.' He laughs, and then there's a moment of silence, followed by, 'Don't tell me you have a date!'

'Hey! There's no need to sound so surprised. I do have a life outside of the office, you know.'

'Who's the lucky guy?'

Damn it. Now I'll have to admit that it's not that kind of a date.

I'm sure he thinks I'm a bit of a boring, computer nerd, despite that drunken kiss five years ago, although he often says things like, 'How's your love-life?' or 'Who's the lucky guy you're spending this weekend with?', but he also often tells me I should, 'get out more', and I'm not entirely sure what he means by any of that.

Whenever he's asked about my boyfriends, I've always laughed and said that I love my job and I don't have time to date. He tells me I should make time, and sometimes he looks at me as if he'd like me to make some time for him.

Or maybe that's just wishful thinking on my part. From what I hear, and from things he says, it seems to me he's always got a girlfriend. Not the same one for very long though. And he's never asked me out. Not even when he doesn't have a girlfriend, so I'll simply have to crush on him in silence, from a distance.

Now he'll know just how sad my love life really is.

'My family and some friends are getting together to celebrate my sister's best friend reopening Seascape Café,' I say. 'I think I mentioned it to you. It was a café and bar, overlooking the beach in Norman Landing but now it's reopening tomorrow as a café during the day, and a bar, bistro, and live music venue in the evenings ... and at weekends ... but it's still called Seascape Café and all that's really changing is...' I let my voice trail off because I'm waffling.

'Wow. How exciting. Listen. Don't worry about this. I'll sort it. You go and have fun. You deserve it. As long as you don't mind me getting the whip out with your team, if I need to.'

'No whips needed. My team's great, as you well know. But I can't leave you and them to deal with this problem. Whatever it is. I'll stay.'

'No you won't,' he says authoritatively. 'And I'm not even going to tell you what's happened. So there.' He laughs and blows a raspberry down the phone. 'Seriously, Em, as difficult as it will be, we can manage without you for one night.'

'But you said it was DEFCON 3?'

'Yeah well. The client thinks it's 3 but it's an Italian company, and we all know that Italians can be a tad dramatic. It's probably somewhere between 4 and 5, so not really a problem at all. Just something we need to be aware of. A minor issue. The smallest glitch. Go. We'll sort it. And I promise that if we can't, I'll call you myself and let you know. Bye. Have a good night.'

'If you're sure, Ben, thanks,' I say. But he's already hung up.

I consider dashing along the corridor to his office but we're at opposite ends of the building and someone else is bound to grab me for some reason or another, between my office and his, and I've still got stuff on my desk I need to get done before I leave.

I hesitate for a fraction of a second and then decide he's right. They can manage without me for one night. And I did promise Katie and Nan I'd leave in half an hour or an hour at the most. Besides which, I am never late. Not even when there's a work emergency. If he needs me, Ben will call.

I ignore the little voice in my head telling me how nice it would be to be needed by Ben. But not necessarily for a work-related emergency.

Two

I leave the office later than I hoped so I'm relieved the traffic is lighter than usual. Norman Landing, and my house in Cherry Tree Close, are a good twenty minutes' drive on an average day, but this evening I make it door-to-door in fifteen. Although, needless to say, Katie and Nan called to find out where I was, just as I got in my car. I lied and told them I was only a few minutes away but that back-fired on me when they told me they would wait.

'No!' I shrieked, probably giving the game away about my untruth. 'Erm. It looks like there may be a bit of a hold-up ahead. You go. I'll see you at the restaurant.'

'Don't be late,' Katie said.

'Am I ever?' I hung up and put my foot on the accelerator, so I hope I didn't pass any traffic cameras.

I've never had a speeding ticket in my life and I don't want to spoil my good record. I didn't speed by much, and I was very careful, as always, but nevertheless, I feel a little guilty, because even a few miles over the limit is still breaking the law. Sometimes I wonder why I'm such a goodie-goodie. But then I remember why, and I remind myself that it only takes a second for something to happen that can change your life entirely. Or someone else's. I promise myself I will never speed again.

I dash inside, taking off my suit as I rush upstairs to change, and buttoning up the front of my white and blue floral dress as I come back down a matter of minutes later. I even called for a minicab during that time. It arrives as I race out of my front door. The restaurant is less than ten minutes' walk but the cab cuts that in half and when every minute counts, it's worth the cost.

I hear the clock on the small tower of Holy Trinity Church strike the half hour as I jump out of the cab, and in my haste, I fail to notice the man about to cross my path. Although technically, it's me who crosses his. There's an audible 'bam' as we collide into one another.

'What the F—' He obviously also failed to notice me, but even in his surprise he stops short of finishing his curse.

'I'm so sorry!' I wail, as I peel myself away from his solid chest. 'I'm late. And I'm never, ever late.' And then I stumble but he reaches out and steadies me.

'Hey. Take it easy. Better late than never. Are you okay?'

I glare at my blue, strappy sandals and their six-inch heels. I knew I shouldn't have bought them, although the blue matches the flowers on my dress to perfection. This is my first time wearing them. What was I thinking?

'I'm fine thanks,' I say, glancing up. 'Are you?'

I briefly register the fact that he's tall, broad shouldered, long-legged, and handsome, with an olive complexion, hair the colour of espresso coffee and eyes to match. There's a hint of stubble on his square jaw, and an odd sort of smile on his lips. Lips that were made to kiss.

Our eyes meet, lock, and I'm sure my gasp is loud enough for him to hear. I can hear his. His dark brows draw together and tiny lines form at the sides of his equally dark eyes. I know this man. And he knows me. But it must be fifteen years or more since he broke my adolescent heart.

'Emma?' He says my name as if he's discovered a precious treasure. 'Is it you?'

'Gio?' He is a precious treasure. Even after all these years my traitorous heart does a little dance of joy at the sight of him. 'Yes.

It's me. I'm ... astonished you recognise me, let alone remember me.'

His laugh is music to my ears. 'How could anyone forget little Emma? Although not so little now, I see, but clearly as serious as ever.'

His eyes scan me from head to toe and I'm sure I actually quiver beneath his intense gaze. Now I'm glad I went home to change. My dress shows off my figure, which even if I say so myself, isn't at all bad. I'm even pleased I wore my new sandals. The high heels make my legs look longer.

'Er. Thanks. I think.'

He reaches out and gently sweeps a lock of my dark brown hair away from my face and then, to my astonishment, lets the palm of his hand linger against my cheek for a split second.

'And even prettier than I recall.'

Now my mouth falls open and I stare at him.

'Still the same Gio,' I say once I regain my equilibrium, but I hear the slight hint of annoyance in my voice. 'Still teasing me after all these years. How long has it been? Twenty years?'

A smile lingers on his mouth but he shakes his head. 'Fifteen. But you're right. It feels like longer.'

I clear my throat. 'Wh-what are you

doing here? In Norman Landing, I mean. Not right here.' My laugh sounds like a machine gun.

He raises his brows. 'Haven't you heard? I thought the gossipmongers would be out in force.' He shrugs. 'I've moved back.'

'Moved back? Back to Norman Landing? For good?'

'Or bad.' He grins. 'Whether it's for ever, only time will tell. I have no plans to be elsewhere right now. I'm glad you stuck around. I've already seen one or two of the old crowd and I was wondering what had happened to you.'

'Nothing's happened to me. Oh! Except my mum died.'

How on earth did I forget that? Hell. This man still has the power to make everything else in my life fade into the distance.

There's genuine sympathy in his eyes and he touches my bare arm with his fingers, sending tingles of excitement to every nerve, every fibre, every cell of my body.

'I'm so sorry, Emma. I heard about that. I should've sent a card or something. I meant to, but...' he shrugs again. 'A card just didn't feel right, somehow, and after we lost touch, I wasn't even sure you'd want to hear from me.'

I prickle at the memory of the day we

parted. The day he walked out of my life and said he would not be coming back. The day he broke my fifteen-year-old heart, and I couldn't tell a soul about it. Not even my friends, and especially not my family because Katie and I had been forbidden from seeing him, and I couldn't let Mum or anyone, know what he and I had been doing behind everyone's backs.

'A card might've been nice,' I say, 'but hey. Erm. How have you been?'

'Good,' he says. 'I've been good.' His smile is devilish. 'In almost every way.'

My ringing phone startles me but I stare at him trying to read his mind.

'That'll be your date wondering where you are,' he says, nodding towards my handbag. 'You'd better answer it.'

I sigh in annoyance. 'It'll be Katie or Nan. I don't have a date.' I check my phone in any case as I suddenly remember it could be Ben. It's Katie, so I ignore it and slip it back into my bag. 'And it seems you're still telling me what to do even after all these years. It was lovely to see you again, Gio, but as I said, I'm late. Look after yourself.'

'Oh. Yeah. You too. It was really great to see you, Emma. Enjoy your evening.'

'Thanks.'

I hurry towards the door of Alberto's, avoiding his eyes, but annoyingly he's there before me and he opens it. There's a huge smile on his face and mischief in his eyes.

'Say hello to Katie and Nan for me.'

'Will do,' I say, as I sweep past.

But we both know I have no intention of doing any such thing.

Three

'You're late!' Katie points an accusatory finger at me, but I'm really not in the mood.

'Tell me something I don't know,' I say, somewhat churlishly. And then I feel guilty for snapping at her as I glance at the faces around the table. 'And yet I'm still here before Tori and Mack. What a surprise.' I force a smile.

Nan squeezes my hand as I sit beside her. 'Is everything all right, sweetheart? You look a little ... flustered.'

'Everything's fine, Nan.' I still sound a trifle testy, so I cough to clear my throat, hoping the process will also clear my mind of thoughts of Gio.

If only it were that easy. Fifteen years absence hasn't rid me of thoughts of him so as if one tiny cough could do so.

Over the years I've often wondered where he was, if he was happy, if he was married. More frequently when he first left, and less so after I met Ben, but I've never been able to forget him entirely. I even had to ask myself, on more than one occasion, whether I found Ben attractive because of his looks, because of the striking similarity to the Hollywood star, or because of his slight resemblance to Giovanni Russo. Gio's hair is a little darker, as is his complexion, but they're around the same height and build, and they have the same intense gaze. They're also about the same age, give or take a few months.

'Well you're here now and you look beautiful.' Nan smiles as she releases my hand. 'Forget about work, relax, and have a good time.'

I try hard not to glance towards the door but like my heart, my eyes betray me, and when it opens, I suck in a breath. But it's Tori who saunters in with Mack, and Gio is nowhere to be seen.

Katie, who is sitting on the other side of me, nudges my arm. 'You only just beat her. What held you up? Work, as usual?'

I almost laugh at her choice of words. If only she knew.

'Actually no. I ... someone bumped into me on the pavement outside and we ... chatted for a few minutes. I would've been right on time if it hadn't been for him. For the person on the pavement, I mean.'

And once again, Gio is shouldering the blame for something that was really my fault.

'Right.' She's giving me one of her, 'there's more to this story' looks, but thankfully Tori plonks herself dramatically on the chair opposite Katie and commands everyone's attention.

'Who knew work could be so exhausting and yet so much fun?' She smooths back her long blonde hair in a manner oddly reminiscent of the famous muppet, Miss Piggy. 'I swear I completely lost track of time and if it hadn't been for Mack, I'd still be slaving over my desk, sorting out a pile of invoices. Now I know why you work such long hours, Emma. Although being my own boss means it's a bit different, of course.'

'Of course,' I say. 'Are you ready for the big day, tomorrow?'

She nods enthusiastically as Mack sits beside her, says a quick 'hello' to everyone, and places his arm around her shoulder.

'Yes. Thanks to Mack, and also to Lou and Dave, and everyone else who has helped me, including all of you around this table. I can't wait for tomorrow. I don't think I've ever been so excited about anything in my life. Oh. Apart from you, my darling.' She kisses Mack briefly on the lips as everyone tuts, or laughs, or shakes their heads, good-naturedly.

I can't believe how much the woman has changed in the last few weeks. She's gone from being a virtual sloth where work was concerned to an absolute dynamo. But as she says, being her own boss makes a difference. And having a man like Mack as a boyfriend has also helped. Not only is he gorgeous, he's kind, considerate and thoughtful, and he knows a lot about property, local authorities, and rules and regulations, so he's been a rock for her to lean on.

She once worked at this restaurant, as a waitress, along with my sister, Katie. Then they moved to London and she went to work for a music label in the A&R department. She's loved music all her life and was hoping to become a mover and shaker in the industry but that didn't work out the way she hoped. Mainly, it has to be said, because she had more than a little rose-tint on her invisible glasses, and also because she seemed to have an allergy to hard work. She also believed she could do whatever she liked, including taking time off, making defamatory remarks about the CEO, divulging confidential information, and finally, behaving in a manner the company, and even the police, disapproved of.

And yet, losing her job as an executive assistant was the best thing to happen to her. She came to stay with Katie for the Bank

Holiday weekend at the end of May, and spent quite a bit of time at Seascape Café. That was where she met Mack, and he was actually the one to put the idea into her head.

We all knew the owners of the café, Lou and Dave, and had done for years, and we also knew the rumours of them wanting to retire, but Mack was the only one to see that there was an opportunity for Tori to make her dreams come true.

How it all came about is a long story, so I won't go into details, suffice to say she had a chat with Lou and Dave and they agreed to sell her a large share of the business.

They remain involved, but in more of an advisory capacity, as they plan to travel and have some fun. They are in their seventies, so it's time.

Tori's studio flat in London was snapped up for the asking price within days of going on the market, and her parents have also contributed some cash towards her new venture.

Lou and Dave have moved out of the flat above the café, and Tori has moved in. Mack, who is officially living with Vida, his aunt, in Seacroft Cottage, a stone's throw from Seascape Café, spends most nights in the flat with Tori, so Katie says. No one who knows them thinks it'll be long before he moves in with her.

Vida is also here tonight because although this evening is to celebrate Tori's new business venture and the reopening of Seascape Café, Mack's been instrumental in helping Tori get the new business up and running.

From tomorrow, not only will Seascape Café be the place to be for anyone wanting refreshment during a day on the beach, or cocktails and a delicious meal in the evening, or a hearty, all-day breakfast, it will also be the premier venue for anyone wanting to be discovered in the music world.

There's going to be open mic sessions, and open-air concerts on the deck and on the beach. The local council have agreed to all the plans so far. And, thanks to Aaron's sister, Meg, pop icon Lucinda Revere is going to be the headline act at the first Seascape Café and Norman Landing Beach Concert, scheduled for the last weekend in July. Meg's boyfriend Rick is the best mate of Lucinda's husband, Cody, and Meg herself is now Lucinda's friend.

It really pays to have contacts in the music industry and Lucinda is the best contact anyone could hope for. Before too long, Tori may well have the sort of clout she has always dreamed of having.

Life has a funny way of sometimes giving us what we truly want but in a manner we had never even considered.

That happened for my sister, too. And for Nan. And for Meg.

I wonder if it will ever happen for me.

Tori leans across and taps my hand. 'Ooh by the way,' she says, grinning, 'before I get too wrapped up in the excitement about tomorrow, was that the gorgeous hunk, Giovanni Russo I saw you with outside? I didn't realise you knew him. He came to the café earlier today and I must confess, I hardly recognised him.'

Now all eyes are on me.

'Giovanni Russo? Is he back?' Nan's astonished tone reveals I wasn't the only one who didn't know.

Katie tenses visibly and shifts on her seat. 'Shush,' she says, leaning forward. 'Don't forget he's a distant cousin of Silvio's.' Silvio is Alberto's son and he now runs the restaurant in which we're sitting, Alberto having supposedly retired. But every time I've been here since the 'retirement', so has Alberto. 'I was going to mention that I overheard Silvio and Alberto discussing him the other day, but it completely slipped my mind. I haven't seen him yet though. And of course Emma knew him. Don't you remember she used to follow us all around? Until Mum told us in no uncertain terms that she didn't want either of her daughters anywhere near the Russo boy.'

'Oh yeah.' Tori laughs.

'So it's true?' Nan looks a tad concerned.

'Yep,' says Tori, looking at me once again. 'He's back. Was it him, Emma? I only saw him briefly as we walked here, but I did see him open the door for you. So...?'

'What?' I say, helping myself to a piece of bread from the basket on the table while my brain whirrs trying to think of a suitable reply.

'Who's Giovanni Russo?' Mack asks. 'And where was I when he came in today?'

Tori turns to him and smiles. 'Aww. You sound a little jealous. No need. He's no one special.' She darts a look at Katie. 'Although I must say, Katie, he's even more good-looking now than he was all those years ago.' She turns her attention back to Mack. 'He's just someone Katie and I, and several others of our age, used to hang around with in our youth. A miscreant from our past.'

'He was *not* a miscreant!'

I hadn't meant to state that so emphatically. But I didn't stand up for him fifteen years ago; the least I can do is stand up for him right now.

Four

The house feels so empty now; something I never thought I'd say. But since Nan and Donald moved into their bungalow three days ago, the place is deathly quiet. I haven't seen much of them, or of anyone really, since that night at Alberto's five days ago. Everyone's been so busy. But we have all been texting one another.

Katie's been working overtime at Alberto's where she's once again a waitress having returned from London in December with no money and no job after her then boyfriend Callum Blake lost everything, and then dumped her.

Aaron's been on-shift. He's a firefighter based at Norman Landing Fire and Rescue and he works two days, two nights then has four days off. But they are so short staffed at the station that everyone has been doing overtime.

Nan and Donald have been unpacking

and generally sorting out their new home. We're all going round this Sunday for a little moving in party, which, weather permitting, will be a BBQ in the garden.

Tori and Mack have been working all hours at Seascape Café and things seem to be going even better than any of us expected – and we all had high hopes for the place. Apparently it's been packed to the gills and they've had to turn people away. But the weather has been perfect for outdoor entertainment, and who doesn't like to hear some music with their glass of wine, or beer, or cocktails?

But Mack will soon be starting his new contract with Trulove Hotels, if things go to plan, so what Tori will do without his help is anyone's guess. Although as his new position is progressing a potential development of Conqueror's Court, and he'll be managing the project from start to finish, meaning he'll be working in Norman Landing for the foreseeable future, and his contract is renewable for the next three years, he won't be miles away.

Plus, Tori has asked Katie to come on board with her and although Katie is still considering it, I think she'll probably agree. It's not quite Katie's dream of running her own restaurant, but as she told me herself a couple of weeks ago, it's as close as it's now likely for her to get. And she and Tori have worked together before, at Alberto's.

In truth, I think Katie's only worry is whether the 'new' Tori is here to stay. And by that I mean, she's waiting, as we all are, to see if Tori will revert to her lackadaisical ways.

That sounds harsh and perhaps a little mean, but until last month, Tori had never shown much interest or enthusiasm for anything vaguely work-related. The 'new' Tori could conquer the world, so we've all got everything crossed that that's precisely what she does.

I haven't seen my besties, Nuala and Mo, either. Nuala works as an NHS nurse in the main hospital in Brighton, which is fifteen minutes' drive away or maybe a little more, but she's recently handed in her notice, and is leaving at the beginning of July. She works almost as many hours as me and she also works shifts, so meeting up with her takes careful planning. Mo, which is short for Monica, is a teacher at a school in Brighton, so meeting up with her should be easier. And yet it isn't.

I've been working such long hours that I've hardly been home at all. The DEFCON 3 situation that Ben kindly handled for me so that I could go to Alberto's that night, was resolved fairly easily, and was, as he had said, closer to a 5 than a 3 and was more about the client's reaction than the actual problem itself. Sadly though, another new client company didn't react to an issue with other software they were running, and that resulted in a major glitch with the new software. Thankfully, one of my own team picked it up and managed to create a patch, then fix the issue, thus averting the likelihood of fallout on a nuclear scale, or so Ben would have us all believe.

Coming home from a hectic office to a deathly silent house feels strange.

I had lived alone for a little over five years, prior to Katie coming to stay in December, and then Nan joining her, and I loved it.

Okay, maybe not right away. At first, living alone was difficult and I'm not ashamed to admit that I cried myself to sleep a few times. But then again, I had moved from a house filled with people and with love, and then, after Mum died, a house filled with memories, to a flat with things brought from that house – and just me. Which was quite an adjustment.

The real reason I bought a place of my own – the small flat first and then this house last year – was because, after Mum's sudden death and the sale of the family home all four of us had lived in, I needed to plant some roots of my own. To steady myself after the shock of Mum dying. And I needed to prove to myself, and to Katie and Nan, that I could stand on my own two feet.

Nan bought a flat in Conqueror's Court, which was a few minutes' walk from both my flat and also this house, and Katie moved to London with her then boyfriend, Callum, and her bestie, Tori.

But life has a way of slapping us in the face, just when we think we've got everything sorted. Callum dumped Katie, who lost everything, including the flat she and Callum rented, when the restaurant they ran together, closed down. That's why she came back to Norman Landing to stay with me. And just a matter of days later, a fire at Conqueror's Court meant Nan also needed a place to stay. I was in New York, for my job, at the time, so Katie and Nan moved into my house.

And then life gave back some of the things it had taken. Katie and my neighbour, Aaron fell head over heels in love and although some people might think it was all happening too fast, Katie moved in with him at the start of this year. Nan remained with me, and shortly after, Donald joined her. As I've already mentioned, he was supposed to be staying at his daughter's but she's a nasty piece of work and the less said about her, the better.

I was actually looking forward to reclaiming every inch of my own space once they moved out, but although this is only a two-bedroom house, it now feels like a cavernous, empty mansion the moment I open the front door.

And it taunts me. I swear it does. Every time I step into the hall.

'You're all alone, Emma Barr,' it says. 'No one loves you.'

Which is ridiculous. I know that. Firstly, a house can't speak. Secondly, at least two people love me. Katie and Nan. So there, house. Put that in your chimney and smoke it.

Blimey. I'm beginning to talk like Ben.

Oooh! Ben likes me. At least I think he does. And several others do too. I think my besties, Nuala and Mo probably love me. I know I love them. I don't see anywhere near as much of them as I would like. Katie and Nan are right about one thing. I am always working.

Aaron likes me, as does Donald. Aaron's sister Meg and her boyfriend Rick like me. Katie's bestie, Tori likes me. And although we've all only known Tori's new boyfriend, Mack for a few weeks, since he came to stay with his aunt Vida, fell in love with Tori, and decided not to leave, he seems to like me. I could go on, but I won't. Suffice to say, I'm not the unloved, lonely woman my house seems to want to make me believe I am.

Why then, do I feel unloved and lonely every time I close my front door when I get home from work this week?

Is it simply because I have forgotten what it's like to enjoy peace and quiet? To have complete silence in my own home. Nan and Donald weren't exactly raucous, but there was always music playing when they were around, or they were humming, or singing, or chatting, or laughing. Is it merely the camaraderie I miss? Both the office camaraderie and the more intimate camaraderie of home when Nan and Donald were here.

Or is it because I have a crush on Ben, who is out almost every night, with his girlfriend?

Or, God forbid, does this feeling have something to do with seeing Gio again after so many years?

I can't remember the last time I went on a date. I rarely even go out with my friends. I really am always working, plus I travel a lot as part of my job. I spent December in New York, February in Sydney, and most of May, in Toronto.

Something needs to change. But what, exactly?

Should I rent out the guest room?

Hmm. Having relatives, or even friends staying is one thing, but a total stranger? I'm not sure that's such a good idea. What happens if someone moves in and we realise we don't get on? Do I just ask them to leave? And will they go without a fuss?

But then again, I am away a lot. And as Katie and Aaron live next door they can keep an eye on things when I'm not here.

No. I don't think a housemate is the answer.

I amble into the kitchen, take a glass from the cupboard, and the bottle of wine that I opened last night, from the fridge, and pour myself a drink.

I'm turning into a lone drinker.

And someone who thinks their house is taunting them.

Do I have more of a problem than I realise?

I take several glugs of wine and feel a little better. I stroll into the sitting room and collapse on the sofa. Reaching for the TV remote, I channel-hop for a few minutes but can't find anything I want to watch.

I could pop next door to see Katie. I know she's not working tonight. But I remember she said Aaron is also off tonight so they'll no doubt have plans. Nuala and Mo have gone to Brighton to see a film. They asked me to go with them but I said I was working and couldn't get away in time.

I could go to Seascape Café. Tori will be busy, but at least I'd know someone there and I wouldn't feel alone. I haven't been there since it reopened and I really should show my face. To be honest though, I'm tired. Too tired to change and too tired to stand in a packed café cum music venue.

I suppose I could have an early night. At least it's the weekend again soon, and I'll be seeing Katie and Nan, along with everyone else I care about.

Or almost everyone else.

Five

Katie, Aaron, and I, along with Aaron's Westie, Ember, arrive at Nan and Donald's bungalow on Sunday, an hour earlier than everyone else, because we had offered to help them get everything prepared. We've brought several fold up chairs we've borrowed from Holy Trinity Church Hall, which are wedged on the back seat with me, piled in the boot, and strapped to the roof rack on Aaron's car. We've also brought extra wine and beers, and I've made a couple of desserts, and Katie's made some cakes, although we know Nan will have made sure there is enough food to feed the proverbial five thousand. Not that there will be that number of guests.

I'm not surprised to see there is very little left to do. Nan has always been extremely well organised. I think I've inherited that from her.

'Are these for me?' Nan gets a little teary-eyed as I hand her the huge bouquet of flowers.

'No. I just need you to hold them for me while I get myself a glass of wine.' I tut and roll my eyes. 'Of course they're for you. And Donald too.'

She pulls me to her with her free arm and squeezes me tight. It never ceases to amaze me how strong she is for a woman of her age.

'But you've already given us a moving in present, sweetheart! You shouldn't be spending all your money on us.'

'Yes, well, this is just a little extra. And Katie, Aaron and Ember have brought you something too, so it's not just me.'

I ease myself away so that Katie can give Nan a gift basket containing a bottle of wine, a mini, lucky 'money' plant, and a box of chocolates enough for two. Although Katie did say on the way here that in her opinion the chocolates weren't even enough for one, and I have to agree with her. But it's a lovely gift.

Nan hugs her and Aaron and tries to hug Ember, but he's got the smell of something and is sniffing the air, and then he's racing towards the garden where Donald is tending to the BBQ.

'Ember's on his way,' Aaron calls out in warning, and hurries after his dog, but before

Donald has a chance to react, the little devil has jumped up and grabbed a string of raw sausages.

Nan tuts, but she's laughing. 'I told Donald it was too early to start cooking but he wants to test the BBQ to ensure it's working properly. Luckily for everyone, I bought plenty of sausages.'

Like everything else in their 'forever' home, the BBQ is brand new.

Donald lost nearly all of his possessions in the fire at Conqueror's Court. His flat was in the central section which sustained the most damage. Nan's flat was in one of the wings, but everything of hers smelt of smoke.

They decided this was a fresh start and, other than a few treasured possessions they were able to save, or unwilling to throw out, every single thing has been purchased during the last few weeks on shopping sprees, both on foot and online.

They've both thoroughly enjoyed it. Nan said it made her feel like a soon-to-be-bride again; Donald said that wasn't such a bad idea.

So, he also bought her an engagement ring, but only Katie, Aaron and I know about that. He's going to propose to her today.

'If I ask her in front of all our friends and her family there's more chance she'll say, 'yes',' he told us, when he took us to one side after Tori's celebratory dinner at Alberto's.

'There's not a chance of her saying, 'no', I can promise you,' I assured him.

'Are you inviting your son and daughter?' Katie asked in astonishment and concern.

'Absolutely not,' Donald said, but there was sadness in his eyes.

Katie and I were relieved. But it is a shame his children are so unpleasant and unreasonable.

Now we're all laughing as Aaron tries to get the string of sausages from Ember. That dog may be small but the little chap can certainly move when he wants to. Aaron steps on the sausage at the end of the string but all that does is break the sausage away from the others, and squirt its contents all over Aaron's trainers.

Katie, Nan, and I all clap and cheer.

'Well done, darling,' Katie says, laughing hysterically as Aaron removes his trainer, stumbles, and in his haste to steady himself, plants his socked foot in the gooey mess.

Even Ember, who is now resting on the grass with his front paws stretched out guarding the remaining sausages between them, appears to be sniggering. Or maybe that's just his usual facial expression.

'Need a hand?' Donald belatedly asks.

Aaron frowns. 'I need a beer.'

'You can borrow a clean pair of Donald's socks,' Nan offers.

Aaron shakes his head. 'Thanks, but I won't bother.' He sits on the sky-blue, wooden bench – also new, and removes his other trainer and sock and then slips his trainers back on. 'I'll put these in the car and get more chairs.' He holds his socks in his fingers and strides towards the side gate.

'I'd better go and help him,' Katie says, still laughing.

'I'll help too,' I say.

'I'll get him a cold beer,' Nan says. 'And a chilled white wine for us.'

Katie and I walk back through the hall and meet Aaron on the drive just as Daphne and Roger Holt, Aaron's parents, and his sister Meg and her boyfriend, Rick Price, step into view.

'Hello!' Daphne says, as cheerful as always and looking lovely in a summery dress. 'I know we're early but we wondered if you might need some extra hands. Oh. What's happened to your socks, darling?'

'Ember,' Aaron says. And everyone nods.

'Nan and Donald have it all under control,' Katie says, smiling. 'But we could do with some help getting in these chairs.' She nods towards the car.

'How many people are you expecting?' Meg asks, laughing. 'I know Nan and Donald are popular but have they invited the entire town?'

'Almost,' I say. 'How are you, Meg? I haven't seen you since the Valentine's Day dance in Holy Trinity Church Hall. Hello again, Rick.'

'Hi, Emma,' they say in unison. And then Meg adds, 'We have been back a couple of times, but you were away on business on both occasions. We're great, thanks. How about you? Still working every hour under the sun?'

I smile and nod. 'But I'm not working today.'

'Who told you that?' Katie says, handing me a chair.

I shake my head and laugh. 'At least I'm not in the office.'

'Leave this to us men-folk,' Rick says, winking as he takes the chair from my hands.

Surely he knows what Meg will say about that?

And yet she doesn't say what I expect.

She smiles, blows him a kiss, links arms with her mum and Katie and says, 'Come on, Emma. They need to show us how strong they are. Let's leave them to it and get a glass of wine.'

Well if Meg Holt isn't going to argue that women are just as capable as men are of moving a few chairs, neither am I.

'Thanks,' I say to Rick, and follow the other women inside, where I see there are glasses of chilled white wine waiting on the kitchen worktop, not just for Katie and me, but also for Daphne and Meg. Nan must have heard them arrive.

After all the hellos are done and dusted, Nan shows Daphne and Meg around the bungalow, which doesn't take that long. Katie and I have been here a few times since Nan and Donald completed the purchase and we've seen it before they had the work they wanted done, during, and after it was finished.

'It's a beautiful home.' Daphne says when they return to the kitchen diner. 'I'm sure you'll both be very happy here. Has Mary mellowed at all?'

She's referring to Donald's daughter because everyone who knows Nan and Donald, knows how difficult things have been with both his children.

Nan sighs. 'Sadly not. Donald puts on a brave face but I know, deep down, their behaviour has broken his heart. He says that this is a new beginning for us and that if they don't want to be a part of our lives, that's fine. He's determined they won't ruin our future. I keep hoping that one day they'll see how awful they've been and, even if they never apologise, that they'll at least accept the situation and come and visit.' She shrugs. 'We can't control how others behave, only how we behave ourselves.'

'Well, here's to you and Donald having long and happy lives together,' Meg says, raising her glass.

We all raise ours and toast, Nan and Donald.

'Thank you, sweetheart,' Nan says.

'We've brought some bottles of bubbly,' I say. 'It's in the boot beneath the folding chairs.'

'What?' Meg gasps in mock horror. 'I'm drinking wine when I could be drinking champagne! I'll tell Rick to forget the chairs and bring in the bottles.'

Nan laughs. 'I should've thought of that. There's some in the fridge. Will you get it, please, sweetheart?' she says to me.

'No!' Meg says. 'I'm joking. This wine is lovely.'

'I know you are,' Nan reassures her. 'But we should be drinking champagne. You're right. After all, this is a very special occasion. Let's have another toast once the chairs are in the garden.'

'In that case,' Katie says, 'I'll ask Aaron to find the bubbly. It needs to go in the fridge.'

She marches towards the front door and when she opens it, a warm breeze wafts through – along with Tori, together with her parents, Chrissie and Lawrence. Vida is also with them, as is Walter, Vida's Golden Retriever. He dashes into the garden the moment he spots Ember, who to my astonishment, still has a few of those sausages. He's sitting in the shade, beneath a large, apple tree and he allows Walter to join him. There's no sign of Mack. I assume he's helping with the chairs.

'Happy new home!' Tori yells, waving a bottle of something in the air. Her voice is so loud that Donald hears her from his spot at the BBQ, shouts back his thanks, and gives a cheery wave.

'Was that a bit loud?' she asks, grinning.

'I've gone deaf, darling,' her dad says, pulling a suitably expressive face. 'I wish I'd helped with the chairs, now.'

I haven't seen Chrissie and Lawrence for ages. Probably not since New Year, but we all know each other well, and are close. They lived in the house next door to our family home for many years, which is how Tori and Katie became best friends, as did our mums. Then they moved to Brighton, and from the fuss both Katie and Tori made, anyone would've thought they had moved to Mars instead of about fifteen miles away.

Daphne and Meg have met them a few times, and they've also become friends, as, it seems, has Vida. I suppose Tori introduced them the minute Chrissie and Lawrence returned from their latest trip. They always seem to be on holiday. But who can blame them? They're both retired and, until recently, Tori was living in London and only saw them some weekends, and on high days and holidays. Besides, although they're not loaded, they're definitely well-off.

We're all exchanging greetings when Katie reappears, and Mack is with her, carrying the box containing the champagne. She must've grabbed him as he arrived, and he's now searching for somewhere to rest the box. Nan's kitchen diner is large but it's getting pretty crowded, especially with all the good luck cards, presents, and bottles of wine piling up on one of the worktops.

'Why not go outside?' I suggest. 'I'm sure several chairs will be in position by now and it's such a gorgeous day. We should make the most of it.'

There's not a cloud in the sky and the sun is high, but thankfully, not the humidity. A gentle breeze is making this the perfect, summer day.

'That's a good idea,' Daphne agrees.

'Where do you want these?' Mack asks, and Katie points to the large, American style fridge freezer.

Nan, Katie, and I remain in the kitchen

diner while everyone else heads out into the long, wide garden. It's bordered with well-established plants, shrubs, and trees and the grass has been mown into stripes. The Indian sandstone patio, that runs the entire width of the rear of the bungalow, is level with the lawn. There's just one broad step down from the kitchen diner, via the concertina doors that are currently folded open.

'All the chairs are out,' Aaron says, joining the three of us still in the kitchen diner. 'And look who I found.'

He steps aside to reveal Lou and Dave, and behind them, several others I recognise as former residents of Conqueror's Court, and friends of Nan's and Donald's.

Now it really is packed in here, so this time I suggest that Nan joins Donald in the garden, along with all their guests while Katie and I finish up. Aaron ushers everyone out but Nan hangs back.

'We were going to open some champagne,' she whispers. 'Do we have enough? I'd forgotten we invited so many people.'

'Yes. If we don't fill the glasses too full,' says Katie.

'I can nip out and get some more,' I offer. 'This is a celebration after all and we don't want to skimp, do we? Especially not today.' I wink at Katie but her brows crease as if she's not sure why. 'Oh. But we came in Aaron's car.'

'Did I hear my name?' he asks.

'Emma's offered to get more bubbly,' says Katie. 'But you'll have to take her.'

He frowns for a second and then smiles. 'Will I ever get that beer?'

'You can have two when you get back.' Nan beams at him.

'And I'll buy you an ice cream,' I say.

'Let's go. Conqueror's Convenience Store or Asda?' Aaron asks.

Both are equidistant from here and only a couple of minutes' drive, but I choose the local store. It's owned by Mr and Mrs Williams, who are lovely people, and they have a wonderful selection of cards. When I mention the cards to Aaron as we get into his car, he too frowns, as Katie did.

'You gave Nan and Donald a card,' he says.

'A New Home card, yes. But I've realised that Donald is supposed to be proposing to Nan today. Wouldn't it be lovely to have a 'Congratulations on your Engagement' card ready, for after she says yes?'

'Assuming she does say yes.'

I tut at him. 'Of course she will.'

He clears his throat. 'I've been thinking of asking Katie.' He shoots me a sideways look. 'What d'you think? Too soon? I've discussed it with Meg and she thinks it's fine, but you know Katie better than anyone. She was with Callum for five years and they never got engaged.'

'Actually, they did. For about a nano-second.'

He frowns again. 'Oh yeah. Thanks for reminding me.'

Callum turned up on Christmas Eve and proposed to Katie on my front lawn, which was covered in snow at the time. She was so surprised, she said yes, even though she had already fallen in love with Aaron. I was still in New York when that all happened, so I only know what Nan and Katie told me later. But that's another story.

'I think I'd better get two congratulations cards, because Katie will absolutely, categorically, without any hesitation, say yes. And this time she'll really mean it.'

I wink at him, and the smile on his face would make the Cheshire Cat look miserable.

In addition to the champagne, I buy two cards for me, and a card for Katie and Aaron to give to Nan and Donald, plus an ice cream for Aaron, who is still beaming as he pushes the trolley around the store, clearly in a world of his own.

'Have you got a ring?' I ask as we head back.

'For Katie?'

I laugh. 'Are you planning on proposing to anyone else as well?'

He grins. 'Nope. And yes. I ... I bought it months ago.'

'Wow! Then why have you waited?'

'Because although I'm sure Katie is the one for me, I wanted her to be certain I'm the one for her. Technically, after Callum, I'm the rebound guy.'

I laugh again. 'Oh, Aaron. You're an idiot. Katie is head over heels in love with you and you are definitely the one. You need to ask her right away. But not today. Today is Nan and Donald's day.'

'Yeah, I – Oh crap! Isn't that Donald's daughter?'

We both turn our heads as we pass the woman standing at the edge of the pavement waiting to cross the road.

'Bloody Hell! It is. What on earth is she doing here? And where does she think she's going?'

'I may be an idiot,' he says, 'but even I can guess that.'

Six

'Mary!' I shout as soon as Aaron stops the car and we both tumble out in an attempt to block her path. 'What are you doing here?'

She's clearly as shocked to see us as we are to see her but she soon recovers herself and juts out her already pointed chin.

'It's a free country. I can go wherever I want.'

'That's true,' Aaron says, far calmer than I could manage. 'As long as it's not to Nan and Donald's new home. It may be a free country but there are laws against trespassing, and if you set foot on their drive, that's what you'll be doing. Unless, of course, you've come to give them a moving in gift and a good luck card. Is that what you're doing?'

She narrows her eyes at him and purses her lips.

'Oh I've got a moving in gift for them, all right, but good luck isn't what I'll be wishing them.'

'For goodness' sake, woman!' I've had enough of her. 'Can't you just accept that your dad is entitled to live his life the way he wants? Can't you be happy for him instead of doing everything in your power to try to make his life – and yours, miserable? You won't win, you know. Ever. No matter what you do, he and Nan will stay together and they'll be happy. The only one who you're going to hurt if this continues, will be you. And possibly your brother. Because although Donald still loves you both, even he has a limit. He won't be around for ever, you know. And when he's gone, you'll miss him terribly. You'll regret all the nasty things you've said and done and wish you could turn the clock back. Go home, Mary, and think about that. We're having a celebration today and if you hadn't behaved so dreadfully, you could've joined us. But if you set one foot on their drive with any intention of spoiling their day, there are several people in their house who will ensure you don't get any further. Now go away. Before I forget that I'm not a violent woman, and I knock you out myself!'

She gasps so loudly when I finally finish my tirade that she actually stumbles backwards. Aaron is grinning at me, I can see that from the corner of my eyes but I continue to glower at Mary.

'Fine! But this isn't the last you'll see of

me.'

'Actually,' says Aaron, 'I sincerely hope it is. For your sake as well as ours. Unless you have a change of heart. Because as Emma just said, there are several people who will ensure you don't get any further. Not just today, but if you ever show your face here again.'

'I'm not scared of you,' she says, but her tone suggests otherwise, and she turns on her heel and stomps back the way she came.

'Phew,' I say, taking several deep breaths. 'I don't know where that came from.'

Aaron smiles. 'Well it seems to have done the trick. For now at least. I wonder if she knows which bungalow it is. Let's wait until we're sure she's out of sight, just in case.'

There were no sale signs up throughout the process, but Mary could have looked on one of the properties for sale sites. Or someone could have told her. She knows lots of people in the town. But Aaron's right, so we wait for a few moments until we're sure and then we get back in his car and drive the few feet to the bungalow.

'Should we tell them?' Aaron asks as we open the front door.

'No. I think we've dodged the bullet, and as I said, we don't want to spoil their day. We can tell them tomorrow, perhaps.'

53

'Tell who, what?' Katie is waiting for us, a bottle of cold beer in one hand.

'Is that for me?' Aaron asks, beaming at her.

'Well it's not for Emma. She's not a beer lover.'

He kisses her on the mouth and then says, 'I love you, Katie Barr.'

'You'd better. Because I love you more than I ever thought possible.'

'Oh get a room, you two,' I laugh. 'Are we opening the champagne now?'

I toss her the card I've bought for her and Aaron to give to Nan and Donald. She stares at it and then laughs.

'I'd forgotten about that! Wait. What if he's changed his mind?'

I tut at her. 'As if that's likely. Aaron? I think you should be the one to ask him.'

Aaron grins. 'I would, but he's not my type and besides, I love Katie.'

'Funny man. Don't give up the day job. Go and ask him when he's planning to pop the question, please.'

'I'm never gonna get to drink this beer, am I?'

'Yes. Take it with you. Now go.'

He throws me a conspiratorial look. 'You're getting awfully bossy, Emma Barr.'

Katie and I get the glasses ready. Luckily, we borrowed some from Seascape Café, and others from my house, and some from Katie and Aaron's, so together with the ones Nan and Donald bought, there should be plenty.

Aaron's back in a moment and he's smiling. 'He's going to do it now, before everyone starts eating.'

'Come on!' I say, pushing Katie outside. 'We don't want to miss this.'

Donald looks at us and nods, and then he clinks a fork against his glass and coughs loudly, but several people continue to talk and only a few take any notice of him. He tries again but he still isn't being heard above the cacophony of voices.

I sigh. 'Must I do everything today?' I mumble so that only Aaron and Katie can hear, and then I clap my hands and yell at the top of my voice, 'Oi, everyone! Please can we all be quiet for a minute? I think Donald has something he wants to say.'

Silence descends and everyone stares at me, and then at Donald, in anticipation.

'Nan,' he says, holding out his hand to her, and she steps forward and takes it. Then he slips an arm around her waist and pulls her close to his side. 'We're so happy all of you have taken the time to join us to celebrate us moving into our forever home, and we both want to thank you for all the cards and gifts and good wishes. If someone had told me that a fire would result in me being the happiest I have ever been, I'm not sure I would've believed them. But that fire meant we could buy this wonderful home together. I don't think many people have anything good to say about Conqueror's Court these days, but it will always be special to me and to Nan, because that is where we met. I knew right away that Nan was someone very special but I had no idea then just how special she would be for me.'

'Aww,' she says, looking him in the eye. 'I feel the same.'

He releases her and moves away and it's obvious she's wondering why, by the expression on her face. When he gets down on one knee, a gasp of excitement escapes her and it also reverberates among the guests. Even Katie and I gasp, and we knew this was coming.

'Our journey together hasn't been as easy as we might have hoped,' Donald says, obviously referring to his children, 'but nothing can break us apart, because we love one another. I didn't expect to fall in love at this time in my life, but being with you has made me feel young again. I'm looking forward to our future together, with wonder and excitement. I love you with all my heart, Nancy Waters. You are without doubt, the love of my life. So, Nan? Will you make me even happier than I thought possible, by agreeing to become my wife? Will you marry me, Nan?'

He produces a velvet covered box, opens it, and sunlight dances on the heart-shaped diamonds. The central one is large, and two either side of that are smaller.

'Oh Donald, darling! Of course I will,' she says.

Tears of joy are visible in her eyes and she bends down to kiss him on the lips as he slips the ring on her finger.

Katie and I look at one another and there are tears in our eyes too. Even Aaron looks a little choked up.

'Now get up, you daft bugger,' Nan says, laughing, as everyone claps and cheers and hoots.

'Erm. I think I might need some assistance,' says Donald, grinning despite his words. 'You make me feel young, my darling, but my bones don't seem to have got that message.'

Seven

I definitely had too much sun yesterday. And without doubt, far too much champagne. I also ate much too much. I danced on the grass in bare feet, and I had a wonderful time, as did everyone else, especially Nan and Donald. But there's one thing that really struck me about yesterday, and I can't get it out of my head. I was thinking about it throughout the night, and I'm still thinking about it this morning.

After most of the guests had gone and only close friends and relatives remained, we sat around the fire pit, drinking cocktails and more champagne and looking at the stars in the darkening sky, and I realised, to my horror, that I was the only person there without a 'partner' by their side.

Even Vida, who had arrived as a single person, or so I thought, was holding hands with a man, who, it turned out, she has known for several months but only recently started dating. Very recently, obviously, because he wasn't with her at Alberto's for Tori's reopening celebration.

So it isn't just my house that thinks I'm unloved and alone. I really am!

Foolishly, because I'd had far too much to drink, I mentioned this to Nan and Katie and ... well, everyone sitting around that fire.

'You haven't met the right person yet, sweetheart,' Nan said. 'Look at us. We're in our eighties and we've just found each other.' She stared at her ring, twinkling in the glow from the fire.

'But you've both been married before. Wait. Are you saying I'll meet someone when I'm eighty?'

'No! Well, maybe. But you'll meet lots of men before then. One of them is bound to be right for you.'

'She won't if she spends her life working,' Katie said.

'She might meet someone at work,' Aaron suggested.

'Or at one of her clients,' said Donald.

'Or at Seascape Café, like Mack and me.' Tori kissed Mack on the cheek.

'Or in another country, like me and Rick,' said Meg.

'We met at a funfair,' said Chrissie.

'I thought it was at the carnival.' Lawrence looked confused.

'Same thing. The funfair was part of the carnival.'

'Oh yes. The Ghost train.'

'The Ghost house,' Chrissie corrected, shaking her head.

'Aaron thought I was stealing his dog,' Katie said.

'Now I'd pay someone to steal him,' said Aaron.

But we all knew he wouldn't. He loves Ember almost as much as he loves Katie.

'This is all very helpful,' I said. 'And it's interesting to know how some of you met, but it doesn't change a thing. I'm still the gooseberry.'

'You can't hurry love,' said Daphne.

'Oh! Someone sang that at the café yesterday,' said Tori.

The café was closed on Sunday because Tori and Mack, and Lou and Dave were at Nan and Donald's party.

'Wasn't that by Phil Collins?' Chrissie asked.

'No.' Tori looked thoughtful. 'It was Luke something or other.'

'I meant originally,' said Chrissie.

Nan shook her head. 'Originally it was by The Supremes. I loved that song.'

And then there were three versions of the song being sung, which turned into a sing-song for the next twenty minutes or so as people started reminiscing about their favourite songs and then suggesting what song Nan and Donald should have for the first dance at their wedding. My love life, or total lack thereof, was completely forgotten.

By everyone except me, that is.

But that was okay. It was lovely to see everyone so happy. I just wish I hadn't had quite so much to drink.

At least my assistant offered to pick me up today, and after swallowing a couple of headache tablets and drinking enough water to empty a small reservoir, I'm feeling slightly more human.

'Good weekend, was it?' Ben asks as I plod into my office still wearing my sunglasses.

He's perched on the edge of my desk and although I'm always pleased to see him, I could do without his cheerfulness right now.

'Please don't tell me we have a situation. I was hoping for a quiet day.'

His grin widens. 'Clearly a good weekend. Anything you wanna tell me? Don't worry, I'm not here because something's blown up. I was just surprised not to see your car when I arrived. You're always here before me, unless you're working on site. But I knew nothing was in the schedule for this week, and there's something I need to tell you.'

My foolish heart skips a beat. He looks

for my car when he arrives? And he knows my schedule? Seriously? Perhaps everyone was right. You can't hurry love. We've been colleagues for the last five years and other than that one, drunken kiss, nothing has happened between us, romantically speaking. Perhaps it just wasn't the right time ... until now.

A vision of a double wedding, with Nan and Donald, pops into my head. I must be more hungover than I thought. As if either Nan or I would want a double wedding.

'Anyway,' he says, sliding rather provocatively off my desk, his gorgeous smile fixed firmly on his handsome face. 'I wanted to let you know that I've booked next week off. I know it's short notice, and I apologise for that, but Honour knows someone who owns their own little island in the Caribbean. Can you believe that? She's arranged for us to go next week. Not the best timing, I'll admit, as we've moving into the rainy season, but the weather is still fairly good out there in June.' He shrugs, but the smile is still there. 'Just the two of us, if you don't include the staff, but apparently, they're uber discreet. Lots of celebrities go there, so they have to be. Imagine it, Em. A week of nothing but sand, sunshine, and sex. I bet you could do with some of that right now, couldn't you?'

He's right on all counts, but it takes me a moment to recover from the shock. It's bad enough that he's still seeing Honour. They've been dating for a few weeks now and he seems to like her. But for them to be going away together, and to a romantic and secluded Caribbean island? I mean, come on! If he'd actually slapped my face for real it probably wouldn't have stung so much.

'Wow. So ... things are pretty serious with you and Honour?'

His brows knit together as if he doesn't understand the question and then he glances out of my window.

'I wouldn't say that. It's a holiday, Em, not a honeymoon.' He returns his attention to me and our eyes meet and hold, and then he clears his throat and turns away. 'Better get on. Need to make sure I don't leave you any minefields that might blow up while I'm away. Shall I get someone to bring you in a vat of coffee? You look as if you could do with it today.'

'Thanks.'

He stops outside my door and pops his head back around it. 'You're still gorgeous, Em. You know that, right?' And then he's gone. No doubt planning his week of sand and sun and sex with sodding Honour.

Eight

I know I said my house feels empty since Nan and Donald moved out and that I'm not entirely thrilled to be living on my own right now, but in truth, the last thing I needed this evening was to find Nan and Katie sitting at my kitchen table with another bottle of my wine, open, along with what looks suspiciously like my home laptop.

'Erm. Is this my house, or have I walked into one of yours without realising?'

'Finally!' Katie says. 'How you'll ever find time to date is beyond me. What time do you call this?'

My eyebrows shoot up in surprise. 'Erm. Time you were both in your own homes. Or at least, time you poured me a glass of my own wine.'

Katie tuts and looks at Nan. 'She's in a mood.'

'Everyone's in a mood on Mondays,' Nan says, pouring me that glass of wine. 'Bad day, sweetheart?'

'You could say that. I love you both, you know that, but I really need to be on my own tonight, if that's okay.'

'No,' says Katie. 'Being on your own is the last thing you need. You said so yourself last night. So Nan and I have hatched a plan to make sure you're not. Stop being a grump and come and sit down. Nan's made you a salad and it's in the fridge so you don't even need to make your own supper.'

That last part is good news. I hadn't realised how hungry I was until Katie mentioned food. The part about them hatching a plan, not so much.

'Is that my laptop?' I ask, heading to the fridge.

'Yes,' says Katie without a hint of hesitation.

'Time to change my password. Or better yet. Please both leave my spare keys when you close my front door on your way out.'

'Don't be silly,' Katie says. 'Now look.'

She turns the laptop round so that I can see the screen as I join them at the table. I'm about to take a mouthful of the delicious looking Caesar salad Nan has made but my hand freezes in mid-air as I see a photo of me, on what appears to be a dating website.

'What the hell is that?'

Katie grins. 'That's you.'

'Funny,' I say. 'I'm well aware that's me. I meant what is a photo of me doing on what seems to be an online dating site?'

'It is an online dating site,' Nan says, as if I need clarification of that point.

'But what is my photo doing on it?'

'It's doing its job,' says Katie. 'You've already got three dates.'

My fork clatters onto my plate and I glare at her.

'I've ... got ...what?'

'Three dates,' she says, unperturbed.

'And that's just on this one,' says Nan.

'This one?' The screech in my voice hurts my throat. 'What do you mean by, "this one"? Are you saying my photo is on other sites?'

'Yes,' says Katie. 'We thought you might need to be on several. You haven't had a date for ages.'

'Oh dear Lord. Kill me now. Are you seriously telling me you've put my photo on several dating sites? Without my permission? And does that mean you've set up a profile for me too?' There's only one line of text beneath my photo and that just gives my first name and my age.

Katie nods in an excited fashion. 'You'll love it. Listen to what it says.'

She turns the laptop back and clicks to another page and then reads aloud what she and Nan have written.

"Hi. I'm Emma. I know everyone probably says this, but this really is my first time on a dating site. I've been single for a while, not because there's anything wrong with me – there's not. Other than I'm a career-driven woman who has to travel a lot for her job. Which means I don't have much time to date, or to meet people in a non-work-related environment. I own my own home. I have a fantastic job. I'm financially independent. All of that might put some men off. But it shouldn't. I have lots of interests and plenty of friends, but I haven't met that special someone to share my life with and I think it's time I did. So why not send me a message and we'll set something up. I'm already looking forward to our first date. See you soon."

'I hate it.' I guzzle my wine in the hope I might drown, and when my glass is empty, I top it up.

'Why?' Katie asks, looking genuinely surprised.

'Why? Oh, where to start?'

'But it's all true, sweetheart,' says Nan.

I open my mouth to speak but decide drinking more wine is a much better use for it. And then, when I'm about to launch into a bit of a rant, my laptop pings like a rapid-fire machine gun, and Katie's face lights up as if there's a halo above her head, or she's won the Nobel Prize for literature, or something.

'Well,' she says, sticking out her chin and smiling triumphantly. 'A lot of men seem to like it. Every one of those pings is another man who wants to meet you. My work here is done. If you're going to be in a mood, I'm going to leave you to it and go home to make love to my boyfriend. Because, unlike you, Emma, I have one. And thanks to me and Nan, so could you, if only you could stop being such a control freak for five bloody minutes and accept that we've done something nice for you. Come on, Nan.'

'Oh!' Nan says. 'Are we leaving? I thought we were going to help Emma choose who to go on a date with.'

'We were. But she clearly doesn't want our help.'

I let out a loud sigh. I know when I've been beaten.

'Okay. I'm sorry. You're right. You and Nan have tried to do something nice for me and I should be thanking you, not having a go at you. Please sit down, Katie. I'll open another bottle and we can look at some of these ... potential dates.' My laptop is still pinging. 'Are those really all men wanting to meet me? Or is my laptop having a seizure?'

Nine

Despite my reservations, and the fact that I really hate the profile Katie and Nan wrote for me, I must reluctantly admit they were right. It has definitely done the job.

Although, as we scroll through message after message, we laugh more than we have for a long time. But we do find a few men who aren't entirely awful. Some actually sound rather nice, and if their profile photos are genuine, and not altered via photo-editing software, some of them look surprisingly good too.

I gasp as I look at one of them. He could be Ben's twin. Except Ben doesn't have a twin, or even a brother. But the man on the site looks exactly like him. His name is Leo and, somewhat cringingly, his profile states:

"Hi. I'm Leo – and yes, I'm as wild and untamed as a lion, but I'm looking for the right woman, with or without a whip, to tame me. People always say I resemble a famous

69

actor, but this is no act. I'm genuinely looking for that one special woman to share my den and to be my pride and joy. Could you be the one to make me roar just for you? If you're ready for me to make you purr, just send me a message. I can promise you won't regret it."

'Oh my God,' I say, after Katie reads it out. 'Did you write that profile too?'

She pulls a face. 'It's crap of course, and oh so cringe-worthy, but you know what? If I didn't have Aaron, I'd send a yes to this guy's message.'

'You wouldn't?'

At least his message isn't as bad as his profile. All it says is:

"Hey, Emma. I like the look and sound of you. Wanna meet up and see if we like each other? Send me a 'yes' and I'll get right on it. Hope we'll both be saying, 'Yes! Yes! Yes! very soon."

She nods. 'I would.'

'Me too,' says Nan and flutters her eyelashes. 'He sounds a bit of a beast, and I bet he's good in bed.'

'Nan!'

'Or he thinks he is,' says Katie. 'Do you reckon that, 'Yes! Yes! Yes! bit is supposed to be you both reaching a climax?' She screws up her nose but she's grinning.

'Or a reference to that scene in '*When*

Harry met Sally.' You know the one,' says Nan.

We all do. That was one of Mum's favourite films.

'But in that scene, she's faking it,' I say. 'Why would he refer to that?'

'Perhaps he wants women to know that he also watches romcoms. And that he's got a sense of humour.'

'Hmm. I think there are better ways to do that.'

But I can't deny I'm attracted to him. It's obviously just because he looks so much like Ben.

'He does look like Ben Affleck, the actor though, doesn't he?' says Katie. 'Do you think his photo has been nicked from somewhere? Or edited?'

'You won't believe this,' I say. 'But there's a guy at work who looks exactly like this one. And I mean, exactly like him. And, to top that, his name is actually Ben Affleck. Like the actor. But in the five years or so we've worked together my Ben has never had any trouble at all finding women to date, so this man isn't him. And my Ben is lovely so he wouldn't use a fake name. But perhaps this guy has stolen my Ben's photo from social media.'

'*Your* Ben?'

Katie and Nan exchange glances and I

realise what I've said.

'Okay. I've had a crush on a guy I work with, for about five years, so what? But he isn't mine, obviously. And next week he's going on a trip to an exclusive island in the Caribbean with his gorgeous girlfriend, so he's never going to be mine, as much as I might want him to be.'

'Why is this the first we're hearing of this Ben?' Katie sounds genuinely annoyed.

'You've had a crush on him for five years?' Nan says. 'Good gracious, Emma. Why haven't you asked him out?'

'Yeah.' Katie nods. 'I always thought you had your act together as far as romance was concerned. It seems it's you who's been putting on an act. Why haven't you talked to us about this?'

I shrug. 'I don't know. I suppose it's partly because we work together. And partly because it's easier if I don't admit it to anyone. As for having my act together, romance wise, nothing could be farther from the truth. I'm sad to say that once I've 'fallen' for someone, it takes me a long, long time, to get over it.'

I look at Leo's profile and sigh, and without thinking, I send a message saying, 'Yes'.

Katie and Nan gasp.

'Did you just say yes to a date with Leo?'

Katie clearly can't believe it.

'Well done, sweetheart,' Nan says and then grins. 'But maybe you should have said, 'Yes! Yes! Yes!' Then he'd know you're eager.'

'Then he'd know I'm desperate, more like.'

'Let's find some more to say yes to,' says Katie.

It's not long before I've replied to ten messages and I honestly can't believe it.

'This is not how I expected this evening to go,' I say. 'But I think that's enough for tonight. It's almost 11 and it's time I went to bed.'

'Good gracious!' says Nan. 'I had no idea it was that late. I'll call Donald and ask if he'll come and get me.'

'You might not be going to bed alone for much longer,' says Katie, getting to her feet as Nan phones Donald.

Reality dawns on me and I virtually break out in a cold sweat, but I force a laugh and make light of it.

'It's been so long since I've had sex, I'm not sure I'll remember how.'

'I'm sure Leo will help you with that.' Katie winks at me. 'Or maybe you could ask Ben for some pointers. You never know where that might lead.'

'To me being sacked, probably.'

I'm about to turn off my laptop when a

reply to one of my yeses arrives. But it's not from Leo. It's from a man called Tim.

'What does it say?' Katie asks as we all peer at it.

I read it out.

"Hi Emma. I'm so pleased you said yes. I live in Brighton. I don't know where you live but I'm happy to come to your town if it isn't Brighton, or meet somewhere in between. And what would you like to do? Meet for a drink? A meal? Go to the cinema? No. Not a good idea. We can't talk during a film. Okay, I'm rambling. Like you, I'm new to this online dating lark. Is it okay to say lark? I don't mean I think it's a joke. I am genuinely hoping to meet someone special. I'm sure you know what I mean, don't you? It all seems a bit weird, arranging a date with someone via the internet. Anyway, I hope you'll get back to me and won't now just delete this message and think I'm a moron. I'm a nice guy, or so my mum says. Another joke. You can tell I'm not a comedian. I'm actually a doctor. But please don't hold that against me. Sorry. Another lame joke. I'm nervous. I'll stop now. Hope to hear from you soon. Best wishes, Tim."

'He does sound a bit of a moron,' says Katie. 'But he also sounds nice.' She sits back down. 'Okay. What are you going to suggest? I think he should come here. Not here to your home, obviously, but here to Norman Landing. That way one of us can keep an eye on you, just in case.'

'In case of what?' Now I'm a little concerned.

'Nothing. It's simply better to err on the side of caution, that's all. You could suggest Seascape Café.'

'Yeah right. And have Tori butting in every five seconds. Because she would. And she'd be telling the guy stories about when I was young. No thanks.'

'True.' Katie nods.

'What about the pier?' Nan suggests.

'What about the pier?' I repeat.

She grins. 'We always used to meet our dates on the pier when I was young. But it was all so different then. It had amusements and penny slot machines and a little café and a dance hall. Ah, those were the days. Now it's virtually bare. But there is that lovely bar slash Italian coffee shop slash gelataria near the end. It serves the most delicious gelato. Donald and I went there last week just after it opened. Doesn't Alberto's family own it? It's called La Dolce Vita and I'm sure someone said they did.'

Katie nods. 'Oh yes. The pier was closed for so many years that I'd forgotten it's been completely repaired and refurbished. It reopened in April, didn't it? The pier, I mean.

Work was still being done to La Dolce Vita when Alberto and Silvio were discussing looking for someone to run the place. They must've found someone, I guess, if it's now open.'

'So should I tell Tim to meet me at La Dolce Vita?'

'No,' says Katie. 'Tell him to meet you at the end of the pier. That way, if he looks like a frog and not like his profile photo, you can walk away. If you're sitting in a café or whatever, escape might not be quite so easy. If you like him, then you can suggest La Dolce Vita.'

'Okay,' I say. 'That makes sense.'

I type a message back to Tim asking him to meet me at the end of the pier in Norman Landing on Saturday around noon. If that's okay with him. A matter of seconds later a message confirms that's fine. And that he's looking forward to meeting me.

'One down, hundreds to go,' Katie says. 'As you're always so busy at work, we can vet any other responses for you, if you like.'

'Hmm. I'm not sure about that. Your tastes are different to mine.'

'Are you saying you don't find Aaron and Donald attractive?' Katie is glaring at me but I see her lips twitching and I know she's teasing. 'And that you wouldn't date them if they were unattached?'

'Oh I absolutely would, despite the age differences. What I mean is...' I don't really know what to say so I let my voice trail off.

It's actually not such a bad idea. If the response to my profile tonight, on just this one dating site, is anything to go by, I'm not sure I will have time to trawl through all the profiles in search of that one special catch.

'We can chat about that another time,' Nan says. 'I think that's Donald car.'

I close my laptop and walk Nan and Katie to the door.

'Any chance of a lift?' Katie jokes.

She only lives next door with Aaron but Nan nods. 'We'll see you safely home.' And then Nan pulls me into her arms and hugs me. 'I've had a lovely time. Goodnight, sweetheart.'

'Me too,' I say. 'Sorry about being stroppy earlier, and thanks for your help with ... everything. You too, Katie. Oh. But next time either of you feels like popping round and letting yourselves in, ring the doorbell first. You never know. I might be having sex with someone.'

'Yes! Yes! Yes!' shrieks Katie, tossing her head from side to side as I open the front door to Donald, and his rather surprised expression.

Ten

I don't know why I haven't tried online dating sooner. By Friday evening, as I'm getting ready to leave the office, I've arranged no less than ten dates over the weekend with ten different men. But sadly, I've had no further messages from Leo. Perhaps Nan was right. Maybe I should have answered, Yes! Yes! Yes!

I wonder if I should tell Ben about the profile photo of Leo, on line. You hear of people stealing another person's identity all the time, and 'new' accounts are always popping up on social media where scammers have 'stolen' someone's genuine photo and set up a fake account. What if this Leo guy has stolen a photo of Ben and is using it to defraud unsuspecting women on a dating site?

I mean, Ben is the spitting image of the famous actor, which itself is pretty amazing. What are the chances of there being yet another man who looks identical to them both?

The problem is, if I tell Ben about Leo then Ben will know I'm on a dating website. He already thinks I'm a saddo, do I want to prove him right? Although what is wrong with being on a dating site? I'm a busy person. I have a hectic life. My career is my priority. I don't get a chance to meet men in the same way that others do.

Yet even as I try to convince myself of that, I know it's not true. People meet their partners in supermarket aisles, or in hotel lobbies, or walking down the street. I've never met anyone like that. Maybe the entire dating process is purely based on luck. You're either lucky enough to find 'The One', or you're not. Clearly luck is not on my side.

But as for Ben, and Leo's online profile, I'll wait a few days. If Leo replies, I'll soon find out if he's real or not. Because if we arrange to meet, I'll see what he's like in real life. He'll either look like Ben, or he won't. He can hardly turn up in a mask. But if he makes excuses and delays meeting up, the chances are, he's a scammer. Then I will tell Ben. Perhaps. Or I might just report the fake guy to the dating site.

I'm speaking on my office phone when the real Ben strolls in, smiling, a little after 6 p.m. and, obviously realising it is a client on the call, he silently points to the two chairs situated on the other side of my desk. When I nod, he stretches out his long, lithe body on the one directly opposite me.

His presence makes me forget what I was saying and as I apologise to the client, I see Ben's smile broaden, as if he knows precisely the effect he is having on my equilibrium.

I can feel his eyes on me, even when I spin my chair around so that I have my back to him. In fact, I think that's worse, because now I'm imagining all sorts of things involving Ben, me, and this chair, so I quickly spin back only to lock eyes with him as he leans across the desk towards me.

'Call me if there're any problems, Clive,' I say, unable to drag my gaze from Ben's. 'You know I'm always here for you. Have a great weekend.' I take a deep, calming breath as I hang up. 'Hi, Ben. What can I do for you?'

He raises his brows. 'If that's a serious question, I can give you a list. And not one thing on it will have anything to do with work.'

I cough and shuffle some papers, and then silently curse my own stupidity. One of the sheets of paper is a print out from the dating site, listing all the men I'm meeting, and I've written the time of the date, beside each one. And now it's on the top. I can read papers upside down. It's one of the things you learn to do when you work in an office. I know Ben can do it too, and from the look in his eyes and the now humongous smile on his face, he has.

'Busy weekend?' He leans back in the chair and stretches out again, resting his elbows on the arms, and forming an upside down 'V' with his fingertips pressed together.

I quickly stuff the print out in my handbag. 'A bit.'

'And taking work home with you? You really should make time to relax and have some fun.'

'I intend to.'

'Hmm. Speaking of relaxing and having fun, I just swung by to wish you a good weekend, and an equally good week without me. Caribbean island, here I come!'

'Oh yes! I forgot you're going away.'

If he believes that he'll believe anything. Apart from my ten dates, I've thought of nothing else this week but him, on a white sandy beach, frolicking in the gentle waves of an azure sea ... with bloody Honour.

Actually, that's not entirely true. I've also thought of someone else. Someone tall and broad with long legs, olive skin, and hair and eyes the colour of espresso. Hot and strong and steamy, espresso.

I shake my head and clear my throat. I

must get a grip.

'You okay, Em?'

'Fine, thanks. Just thinking of all the things I've got to do, that's all. Well. You'd better be off, hadn't you? You don't want to miss your flight.'

He studies me for a moment and neither of us speak. I shuffle more papers and then I look across at him and he's still staring at me, but in a way he's never done before. Almost like he's torn, and he doesn't want to get up from that chair, flight or no flight.

And then, just as I think he's about to say something, my mobile rings, startling me.

Ben sits upright and runs a hand through his hair and then jumps up from the chair, throws me a brief smile and heads for the door. I let my phone continue to ring as I watch him, and I hold my breath as he turns, looks at me, and smiles again.

'I'll miss you, Em,' he says, and there's an odd catch to his voice, but before I have a chance to speak, he's gone.

'What?' I snap, when I answer my phone, without even looking to see who's calling.

'Hey! What's up with you? Is this a bad time?' It's my bestie, Nuala.

'Oh God! I'm sorry. No. It's fine. How are you?'

'Good, thanks. Listen. You know I'm leaving the NHS, right? Well, I've finally got all the products I need to get my kitchen table start up, started. If you see what I mean. I can't wait to try some of it out, sooooo ... I've spoken to Mo, and she's up for it, and I'm hoping you will be too. Are you doing anything this evening? Other than working, obviously.'

'Erm. Katie and Nan are popping round, but I don't have to be with them for long, if you need me.'

'Excellent! Are they just popping in for a chat?'

'Sort of. Yes.'

They are coming round to go over all my dates, what I should wear, emergency codes for me to use if I get into any serious trouble and need to call them to help me out – although if I do get into any serious trouble, the police will be the first people I'll call, not my gran or my sister. We're also looking at some more men who have been in touch on one of the other sites, and who Nan and Katie think might be worth fitting into my schedule. They told me off for calling it a schedule, but really, what else can I call it? I haven't mentioned anything to Nuala and Mo yet, about my foray into the world of online dating. I was going to tell them when I saw them. So that'll be tonight.

'Then bring them here. If they're up for it. The more the merrier.'

'Erm. Okay. I'll ask them. I'm not sure if you've told me, and I've missed it, but what, exactly, is it that you're hoping we'll all be up for?'

'Guinea pigs.'

'Sorry? Did you just say, "guinea pigs"? Are you starting a business breeding and selling small mammals?'

'Yeah. And I've put you down for two. With cages, food, and everything it comes to five hundred and ninety thousand quid. Is that okay?'

'Erm. I know that's obviously a joke but I haven't got the punch line yet.'

She sighs loudly and although I can't see her, I know she's rolling her eyes.

'I'm not selling guinea pigs, you plonker. *You are* the guinea pigs. I'm going to be making skin care products, remember? Soap, face cream, shampoo, and stuff. I told you and Mo about this months ago.'

'Oh! Of course. Phew. I was panicking there. I have enough trouble looking after myself, let alone two awfully expensive rodents. Yes. I'm sure Katie and Nan will be okay with that. Just one teensy question. You have got this stuff from reputable sources, haven't you? And you do know what you're doing, don't you?'

'That's two questions. And the answers to both are, yes. I went on a course last summer. I told you and Mo all about it. I got five stars and a certificate. It's hanging on the wall in my hall. Do you ever take on board anything anyone says if it hasn't got anything to do with your own exceedingly important and time-consuming job?'

'Ouch.' I've upset her. And no wonder. I do remember her telling us about it and I did see the certificate. I bought champagne to celebrate and we drank it in her sitting room. 'I'm so sorry, Nuala. Of course I remember. It just slipped my mind. Forgive me. I love you. I'll bring wine. And chocolate mint fudge ice cream.'

'And a bottle of milk. And some salt and vinegar crisps. And five boxes of tissues. A bumper pack of toilet rolls. The soft ones. Oh, and two tins of Heinz baked beans.'

Nuala drives a hard bargain. Basically, I think I'll be doing her shopping.

'Done. I'm making notes as we speak. What time do you want us to be there?'

'Around 7 p.m. would be good. Mo's got a parent-teacher thing so she's coming straight here from work. So maybe, if you happen to pass Pizza Pie you could pop in and bring us a couple of their Vesuvius pizzas. And whatever you, Katie and Nan want.'

I glance at the clock on my wall. It's already 6.30 p.m. and if I've got to get everything she wants, there's no way I'll make it to her place by 7.00, and I do hate it when people are late. I make a point of never being late, if I can.

'Would 7.15 be okay? Only I haven't left work yet and I need to call Katie and Nan and see if that works for them, plus there may be a bit of a wait at Pizza Pie. It is Friday evening after all.'

'As long as you're here by 7.30, that's okay.'

'Brilliant. I'll see you later then.'

I immediately call Katie and Nan as I leave my office, to tell them of the change of plan and to see if they want pizza – which they do. I call Pizza Pie and place an order to collect, and then I call Mr Williams at Conqueror's Convenience Stores and tell him what I need. He and his wife are great and over the years, we've often phoned ahead like this and he's had the order ready and waiting.

'The only thing I don't have is the chocolate mint fudge ice cream,' he says, as I'm getting in my car. 'But I do have chocolate ice cream.'

'Okay. Thanks. I'll take that.' Nuala won't be happy, but at least it's ice cream.

I'm lucky that, once again, the traffic is light and I arrive home pretty quickly. And without speeding, so I'm proud of myself. I get changed into jeans and a T-shirt, put six bottles of wine in a box, and text Katie to meet me at my car. We head to Nan's, who is also waiting on the drive, and then I stop at the Stores to collect the shopping from Mr Williams. I have to jump out because the order is on my card. And it's the same at Pizza Pie, but Katie gets out too to help me carry the pizzas. Then I drive along Beachland Road towards Nuala's house on the outskirts of town, and as we approach the pier, I slam on my brakes.

'What the hell!' Katie says.

'It's a good thing the pizzas are strapped down,' says Nan, 'or you'd be wearing them all on the back of your head. And Pizza hair is not a good look for anyone. What made you stop in such a hurry?'

'Ice cream.' I point towards the pier. 'Didn't you say La Dolce Vita is a gelataria?'

'Amongst other things, yes, but I don't see—'

'Don't worry. I won't be long.'

I dash along the pier and can see the lime green, white and raspberry striped awning jutting out above a glass frontage surrounded by lime green chairs and tables shaded by raspberry-coloured parasols. I'm puffing by the time I reach the large circular area where La Dolce Vita is situated, but I'm thrilled to see it's open. I wasn't sure what the hours might be, since it's a coffee shop, bar, eatery, and ice cream parlour all rolled into one, as is often the case with Italian establishments like this. But I'm not so thrilled to find the place is packed and there's a queue. Two queues in fact, snaking either side of more lime green chairs and tables.

I hesitate, looking from left to right and trying to see what each queue is for. Is one for coffee? Or ice cream? Is the other for alcohol? Or food? The place serves it all and there seems to be one long counter behind which several people are busy working, so there's nothing to indicate which queue I should join. A couple of people look at me as I stand between the queues and stare at the row of shelves running along the back wall and the long menu board above them offering so many delights and temptations that I'm momentarily transfixed. And then I feel a hand on my elbow and I'm being led outside.

I am embarrassed to admit that, for one ridiculous second, I think I am being abducted or something, and I am just about to scream when I see whose hand is on my elbow.

'Gio! What are you doing here? And more importantly, where are you taking me?'

'Hello, Emma.' He lets go of my arm and looks me up and down. 'I saw you hovering, and it seemed as if you were looking for me. Was I wrong?'

'Erm.' I'm waiting for my skin to stop tingling from his touch, but as it's taking its time I continue. 'I'm afraid so. And I wasn't hovering, I was confused. Why would I be looking for you here? Or looking for you at all, in fact?'

His eyes narrow. 'Because I work here. I thought you knew.'

'You work here? Why would I know that?'

His brows knit tighter too. 'Katie works at Alberto's, right?' I nod. 'Then didn't she tell you?' I shake my head. 'I thought she would.' He shrugs. 'My mistake.' He coughs to clear his throat. 'Do you want to go back in and join the queues?'

'If you tell me which is which.'

'Are you hoping for a table, because we're packed as you can see, but—'

'Ice cream,' I interrupt him. 'I'm here for ice cream. Chocolate mint fudge ice cream, to be exact. Do you have that?'

He glances back inside and so do I. Now I can see a tall display case on the right-hand side of the counter, containing several metal tubs of colourful gelato flavours.

Gio shakes his head. 'No. But I do have the three as individual flavours. I could put them together in one large tub, if that would help.'

'Could you ... sort of mix them together?'

He raises his brows. 'Are you asking me to stir them into one gooey mess? Because that is what would happen.'

'Would that be a problem?'

His hand flies to his heart and he acts as if I've shot him or something.

'Yes. But I'll do it for you, Emma, if I must.'

'My friend likes chocolate mint fudge ice cream,' I say, with a shrug. 'I didn't mean to, but I upset her today so I want to get her exactly what she wants. Ooh! That reminds me. I've got pizzas in the car.'

'Please don't tell me you want those mixed in with the ice cream.'

I laugh. 'Doesn't everyone?'

'Obviously.' His gorgeous mouth quirks into a smirk. 'Are you saying you want me to be quick so the pizzas don't get cold?'

'Well yes. I suppose I am. But we can reheat them.'

'Are they from Pizza Pie?'

'Of course.'

'Then all is forgiven and I'll make your mess...,' he grins, '...ice cream, as quickly as I can. But please, I beg you, do not tell anyone else I did this. Okay?'

'Okay. Thank you. Erm. Do I have to get in one of the queues? Only the pizzas...' I let my voice trail off and I smile at him.

He sighs and shakes his head. 'No. Come with me and we will go in the back way. That way customers won't think you're queue-jumping.'

'Thank you so much, Gio,' I say, following him to the rear of La Dolce Vita. 'I owe you one.'

He glances back over his shoulder and although he doesn't say it, I know I owe him a lot more than one. And he knows it too.

Eleven

'Oh. My. God!' Nuala says, as she licks every tiny speck of ice cream from her spoon. 'This is like licking Heaven. I've never had ice cream like it. Forget my usual chocolate mint fudge. This is now my favourite. Where did you get it from?'

She's not alone is savouring the deliciousness, but as I'm licking my spoon, my mind is wandering back to La Dolce Vita. I stood so close to Gio, behind that display case, that I could almost have licked him. I was tempted, to be honest. My heart was thumping in my chest, tingles were running up and down my body, and tiny droplets of perspiration formed on my red-hot face, every time he looked at me, which seemed to be often, so I babbled about Nuala and her new business.

I told him about the guinea pigs and he said he'd take three. His laugh gave my tingles, tingles, and my heart shrieked, 'Let me out of here! I need to be with his heart in that gorgeous, hunky chest!'

I told him that Katie and Nan were in the car, and I told him a million other things I can't even remember, because I was so busy watching his muscles flex with each movement he made, each scoop of gelato he put into tubs, and the way his hair fell across his temple, and the way his lips parted a fraction and he licked them, that my brain wasn't connecting with my body.

When he put five scoops of Pistacchio (pistachio ice cream) and five scoops of Bacio (chocolate and hazelnut ice cream) into tubs, and our eyes met and locked for a moment, it was as if he was telling me he remembered they were my favourites, and I nearly threw myself at him.

Thankfully, I didn't.

I had to force myself to turn away, in case my self-restraint failed, so, unbeknown to me, not only did Gio give me a tub of the chocolate mint fudge 'mess', and the two tubs of my favourites, he also put a few smaller tubs of different flavours in the La Dolce Vita bag for life he handed me. There was Stracciatella (vanilla with chocolate pieces) Limone (a zingy lemon) and Fragola (like freshly picked strawberries) as I discovered later.

Plus, he refused to take any money from me, saying I could buy him an espresso and a couple of bombolini, one of these days, instead. I remember his favourite filling for the large, Italian doughnuts was *Nutella*, a chocolate-hazelnut spread, with the more usual filling of crema pasticciera, or pastry cream as we would call it, coming a close second, although he often added a squeeze of lemon to his.

'It's from La Dolce Vita, on the pier,' I say. 'But please remember, he did this as a favour, and they don't stock this particular ... flavour. You can buy the three individually and then mix them together like that.'

'I'm going to place a regular order.'

'Me too,' says Mo. 'For all of these.'

'I must admit he makes delicious ice cream,' says Nan, closing her eyes as she has another mouthful of Fragola. 'But then the family always were adept at that. It was honesty that the boy...' She coughs. 'No point in digging up the past.'

We had already done that. When I returned to the car with the ice cream, I asked Katie why she hadn't told me Gio worked there.

'Does he?' She seemed genuinely surprised. 'I didn't know.'

'He seems to think you did.'

'He's wrong. Why would I lie? Perhaps he thinks Alberto or Silvio have told me. But they haven't. As I said the other day, I overheard them talking about the gelateria on the pier and that was it. They didn't mention Giovanni, and they definitely didn't say he would be working there.'

'I didn't see him when Donald and I were there,' Nan said. 'At least ... oh my goodness! Was he the tall, dark, and handsome man who served Donald, I wonder? I waited outside and I certainly didn't recognise him as the nineteen-year-old boy I last saw fifteen years ago.'

'Tori didn't recognise him when he went to Seascape Café, remember?' Katie said. 'She told us that, at her celebratory meal. I haven't seen him yet, but I don't suppose I'll recognise him either.'

'I recognised him immediately,' I said. 'Well, within a few seconds. He's older, obviously, but he hasn't changed a bit.' I couldn't stop the wistful sigh from escaping.

'Is there something you want to tell us?' Nan asked.

'What? No. We'd better go or those pizzas will be cold.'

I revved the engine and sped off, and thankfully, no one mentioned Gio again until we opened the bag for life and saw the selection of ice cream.

'Ooh!' says Nuala, picking up on Nan's words. 'Bit of a bad boy, is he? And Italian, too. If he looks even half as good as I suspect he does, I'll marry him tomorrow and have his babies. Is he single?'

I choke on my last mouthful of Bacio. It must be the hazelnuts. At least that's what I tell myself.

'I have no idea,' I say, when I can speak again.

And I realise that is true. I don't have any idea. Is he single? Is he dating? Is he ... married? Why does that thought depress me?

'Hmm,' says Mo. 'Perhaps a trip to the pier for an ice cream, this weekend, might not be a bad plan.'

'It's a date,' says Nuala. 'Coming, Emma?'

'Bloody hell!' I say, as the full horror of my situation suddenly dawns on me. 'I've got all those dates this weekend! And they're all on the pier.'

How am I going to avoid seeing Gio? Or more importantly, ensure he doesn't see me. What will he think if he sees me with one man after another? Will he even care?

Of course he won't. But I don't want him to think badly of me. Although I suppose that ship sailed years ago when I let him take the blame instead of me. But I did so at his instance. It wasn't my idea or my choice. It was his.

'Dates? What dates?' asks Mo.

I briefly explain that Katie and Nan signed me up for online dating and that I've arranged ten dates.

'Wow,' says Nuala. 'It's about time you did something about your love life. Or lack of it. Not that I can talk right now. I was dating that sodding doctor, until I discovered I wasn't the only nurse he had on the go.'

'Erm. His name wasn't Tim, was it?' I query. 'One of my dates is a doctor.'

'You know it wasn't. You met him. It was Eddie.'

'Oh yes.'

'I'm single at the moment too,' says Mo. 'Perhaps we should sign up to this online dating, Nuala. What do you think?'

'I think we should wait and see how it goes for Emma and then decide.'

'Thanks. So I'm the guinea pig, am I?'

'Yes,' Nuala says. 'And speaking of guinea pigs, I think it's time we tried some of these products. Anyone allergic to anything?'

I shake my head, as does everyone else, although I have no idea whether I am or not.

The boxes of herbs, oils, gels, clay and beeswax, and the lotions and potions Nuala had prepared earlier, are as colourful and almost as delicious-looking as Gio's ice cream. Some smell divine, others ... not so much, but Nuala assures us all, she knows what she is doing and we simply need to trust her. Which, of course, we do.

We spend the next few hours sampling several face masks, washes, and creams, and although a couple of them make my skin tingle – not in the exciting way that Gio does, but in more of a 'oooh, this itches', kind of tingling, I'm not overly concerned.

It is a fun evening with my family and my best friends, filled with love and laughter, wine and delicious food, and I decide I need to spend more evenings just like this one. I only have one glass of wine, as I am driving, but the others make up for my abstinence. It has been a long time since Nuala, Mo and I had spent an entire evening together, and having Katie and Nan there, only adds to our enjoyment.

My face ached from laughing by the time I drove Nan and Katie home. We all made several purchases from Nuala's fledgling skin care range and I even bought a moisturiser and an aftershave from her line of products made for men. Gio had been kind enough to give me all that ice cream, and although I had every intention of treating him to an espresso and bombolini as soon as was humanly possible, I could give him these extra little gifts the following day.

I would take them to him at La Dolce Vita on my way to meet my first date of the day. That would give me an excuse to explain about my dates. Not that I needed an excuse, or that I needed to explain to him what I was doing. My love life was none of his concern. He'd made that abundantly clear fifteen years ago on the day he left.

Nevertheless, as I drove along Beachland Road, I couldn't stop my foot from easing off the accelerator as we neared the pier, and my eyes from drifting towards La Dolce Vita.

It was gone midnight but light beamed through the glass frontage casting a path of creamy white along the wooden boards, just like the path of glistening silver the moon was casting across the sea.

With my window open the smell of salt drifted towards me and I could hear the swish-swash of the waves against the shore. Although my engine was obviously running, I felt enveloped in an odd sort of silence.

I know this will sound ridiculous but it was as if Gio was calling to me, and I really wished Katie and Nan weren't with me, so that I could park the car and go to him.

We would stand at the end of the pier looking up at the vast expanse of sky above, lit only by the moon, and myriad stars twinkling in the blackness. Even at this time of night, or I should say, early morning, the air was balmy and the breeze was warm. I imagined Gio taking my hand in his and slowly easing me towards him, our lips meeting in a kiss so soft and yet so passionate and all-consuming that the universe itself would fade into insignificance.

Twelve

I had the worst night of sleep I've had for a long time. I don't know if it was because of my silly imagination and the dreams I had of Gio, and of Ben, and of a parade of other men, or if it was because my face seemed to be on fire.

I must have got some sleep, because I had those dreams, but I knew that when I looked in the mirror, my eyes would be both heavy-lidded and puffy beneath.

Nothing could have prepared me for the horror my reflection actually throws back at me.

My face looks like a map of Mars; it is red and lined and blotchy with patches of angry raised spots.

What the hell has happened!

It must have been one of Nuala's skin care products.

I hastily dial her number and shriek at her down the line.

'I look like something out of a horror film, Nuala! What am I supposed to do?' I send her a photo of my face. 'Have you had the same reaction?'

'Calm down, Emma,' she says, still half asleep, and very possibly hungover. I hear her gasp at the photo. 'It must be some sort of allergic reaction. My skin feels fine. Hold on while I take a look. Wow! Sorry. My skin looks better than ever this morning.'

'Great! That's just typical, isn't it? The first time in my life I've ever had ten dates, and what happens? The Kraken looks like a beauty queen compared to me. I can't be the only one this has happened to, can I?'

'I'll call Mo. You call Katie and Nan, and then call me back and we'll try to ascertain what might have caused it.'

'Okay,' I say, feeling so dejected that I don't have a better idea. 'But you're a nurse, Nuala. Surely you know how to treat something like this?'

'You'd think so, wouldn't you? But you'd be wrong. I've never seen anything like it. That doesn't mean it's bad. It's simply that rashes weren't something I came across much in the Orthopaedic department.'

Katie says the same as Nuala; that her skin feels fabulous, as does Nan. When I call Nuala back, Mo has told her the same.

'Fantastic! So I am the only one then.

What did I use that the rest of you didn't? And, more importantly, what can I do to get my skin back to the way it was?'

'Erm. I don't think you used anything we didn't. I hate to say this, Emma, but it must be an ingredient that only you are allergic to. As to what you do, I'm not entirely sure. I can come round with some soothing lotions and see if any will help.'

'Thanks, Nuala, but – and please don't take this the wrong way, because I'm not suggesting there's anything wrong with your products – I'm somewhat loathe to put anything else of yours on my face right now, unless you can guarantee it'll help. Clearly, as all of you are fine, it is just me and my skin, but unless we know what caused it, anything we try might only make it worse.'

'I believe tea tree oil could help but I'll check through all my course notes and see if I can find any info on allergic reactions. Other than that, or suggesting you visit your GP ... or A&E, I hate to say this, but I'm not sure I can really help right now. Let me do some research and get back to you, okay? Don't panic. There's bound to be an answer somewhere.'

'Thanks.'

A&E doesn't sound like such a bad idea. But is this classed as an accident? It's definitely an emergency. Although, needing to look good for ten dates with total strangers, might not be considered an emergency as such, by some of the nurses and doctors at the NHS hospital.

I call Nan again for advice, but she's no more help than Nuala. She does sound a little more concerned than my bestie, who is in part to blame for this I feel, did though, it must be said.

Katie, who has popped round to see if she can help, also can't. Her best suggestion is that I try to cover it with makeup. Or cancel all my dates and pretend I've come down with a tummy bug or something.

'Don't tell them your face is covered in a dreadful, ugly rash. Men want to think we women are always beautiful. Although I know Aaron would still love me, even if I looked like you right now.'

'Not helpful,' I say. 'I'm going to the pharmacy. Mrs Williams might have some better ideas.'

Mrs Williams, who owns Conqueror's Convenience Stores with her husband, is also a pharmacist and they have a small pharmacy within the store. I rush to the counter, trying to cover my face as best as I can, and note the look of surprise on Mrs. Williams' face when I step forward after the customer before me has left.

'It's awful, isn't it?'

I'm trying hard to stop the tears from falling. They've been pricking at my eyes since I got up. Unless that's also part of this allergic reaction?

I explain about last night in some detail and she nods until I finish.

'It's definitely an allergic reaction. The best thing to do is to go to A&E. They can give you an injection which will help soothe the itch and calm the redness. You should see a difference within a few hours and within twenty-four to forty-eight hours, you should be as good as new.'

'But I don't have twenty-four hours! And there's always a queue in A&E. I've got a date at 10.00, and another at noon, and one at...' I let my voice trail off as her eyebrows go higher with every word I say.

'I can give you some cream. But again, it won't have any effect for several hours, other than reduce the itching and the redness a little.'

'That's something, I suppose. But is there nothing that might have an immediate effect?' I ask, pathetically, even though she's just told me there isn't.

'A miracle,' she suggests.

I hear a cough behind me. The next customer is growing impatient. But so am I.

'Okay. And where might I get one of those?'

'I may be able to help.'

I recognise the voice behind me and shut my eyes in disbelief. Can this day get any worse?

There is no way I am turning round to face Gio.

'Thanks. But I'll see if I can find a miracle. Perhaps Holy Trinity Church might help.'

He sighs. 'You may as well turn round, Emma,' he says. 'I can see your face in the mirror.'

My eyes shoot to the large, circular mirror hanging at an angle above the pharmacy counter. I had completely forgotten it was there.

Gio waves at me and gives me an odd sort of smile. It's a cross between sympathetic and amused, and I'm not sure if I want to hit him, or laugh at the absurdity of my situation.

'Thanks,' I say again to Mrs Williams, and then I turn to Gio and force a smile, but the tears are welling and I'm not sure how much longer my stoicism will hold. 'Laugh all you like.'

His eyes meet mine as he slowly shakes his head. 'Come with me.'

He takes my hand and the tingling I feel has nothing to do with my rash.

'Weren't you in the queue?' I ask.

'No. I saw you come in and I wanted to have a word.'

I gasp. 'So ... so did you hear my conversation with Mrs Williams?'

He nods.

'All of it?'

He nods again and grabs a wire basket with his free hand.

'Don't you have anything to say about it?'

'Do you want me to say something about it?'

'Erm. Not really. I'm embarrassed enough as it is.'

'Why are you embarrassed?' He hands me the basket. 'Hold this please.'

I take it from him and my face gets redder. If that's possible. He picks up a cucumber and plops it in the basket. I can't believe he's shopping for salad when I'm dying from humiliation.

'Because not only did you hear about how I got this ugly rash, you also now know that I'm meeting ten men this weekend.'

'Ten?'

Now he does look surprised and, as his fingers tighten just a fraction on mine, it's only then that I realise we're still holding hands. My face almost bursts into flames. I ease my hand from his and he watches me intently.

'Yes. Ten.'

'I only heard about three.'

I cough and cast my eyes towards the floor. 'Yes. Well. Katie and Nan set up a dating profile for me last week and ... surprisingly, I got a lot of response, so they suggested I meet the ones I liked the sound of, this weekend ... on the pier... because that's where Nan used to meet her dates ... before she married Gramps, of course. Now I bet you do have something to say, don't you?'

He studies my face for a second, no doubt wondering why even one man would be interested in meeting me, let alone ten.

'Yes. I do. Firstly, I'm not at all surprised your profile got a good response, and nor should you be. Secondly, why do you need a dating website? I would've thought men would be falling at your feet. And thirdly, there is nothing for you to be embarrassed about. It's your life, Emma. You can date as many men as you want. Although ten in one weekend is pushing it. Purely from a timing perspective. What happens if you really like one of them? Do you just say, "I'm sorry but your time is up", and move on to the next one?'

I'm still on the bits where he said he's not surprised I got a good response and that men should be falling at my feet. Does he think I'm attractive? Or is he just saying that to make me feel better? It takes my brain a while to catch up with the rest of it.

'Oh. Erm. I hadn't thought about that. Yes. I suppose that's exactly what I'll do.'

He shrugs and walks on, picking up a bottle of extra virgin olive oil. 'As I said, it's your life.'

Now I'm getting annoyed.

'I thought you said you might be able to help me. I don't want to sound ungrateful, but could you possibly do your shopping later? I've got my first date in three hours' time.'

He quirks a brow. 'This isn't for me,' he says, pointing at the basket. 'I'm getting this stuff for you.'

'Oh. Well thanks. But I don't need a cucumber, and I've got olive oil, so I'm good.'

He laughs. 'For your skin. The cucumber will soothe it and the olive oil mixed with a little oatmeal will help. And then I'll add my secret recipe, and a tub of ice cream, and you'll be amazed at how much better that rash will look in no time.'

'Really? Are you sure? Cucumber and oatmeal? And as much as I love your ice cream, eating another tub of it today will only make me put on weight.'

'You won't be eating it. I'll be putting it on your face.'

'Ice cream!'

Unwanted images of Gio smothering not

just my face but my body in ice cream, popped into my head.

'Yes. Don't you trust me, Emma?'

The way he is looking at me, I don't trust myself.

But I do trust him.

'Yes, Gio. I do.'

After he adds a few more things to his basket, and insists on paying, I drive us to the pier, as per his instructions. We walk to La Dolce Vita, with me making sure I keep a safe distance, because every time he touches me, or his skin brushes against mine, that tingling gets worse. The good tingling, not the bad. And I need that to stop. But when he takes me into a cosy little room at the rear, and tells me to lie down on the small sofa and close my eyes, my imagination runs riot.

And then he begins smoothing an ice-cold paste that smells both odd and yet heavenly onto my face with the tips of his fingers. I open my eyes briefly and his face is so close to mine that if I stretched my neck a fraction, I could kiss him.

'Close your eyes,' he whispers, 'and keep them closed.'

His breath on my neck sends new shivers of delight the length and breadth of my body and I have to bite my bottom lip to stop myself from yelling, 'Yes! Yes! Yes!'

And it wouldn't be a fake sentiment, I

can assure you.

He places something cold and damp on each of my eyelids and then continues to smooth more ice-cold paste onto my face and down onto my neck. His fingers brush across my collarbones and over my décolletage and I hope he's looking at my face because I don't want him to know what his touch is doing to my body. This is both ecstasy and agony and I'm honestly not sure how much more of it I can take.

And just when there's a very good chance of me begging him to move his hands lower, with or without the paste he's using, he stops.

'Now we wait,' he says, and there's a slight catch in his voice.

I wait in silence, save for the sound of his breathing and that of mine.

I don't know what he did with any of the ingredients he mixed together but within a few minutes, my face is no longer itchy and the burning has subsided. I hear him shift in his chair, and he removes whatever was on my eyelids, but he doesn't speak right away.

It's at least thirty seconds until he says, 'Now you can open your eyes.'

When I do, he's leaning back in his chair as if he's been watching me. His long legs are stretched out in front of him and his arms are loosely folded across his chest. The odd smile on his mouth is both triumphant and also sexy and there is a look in his eyes that sends those tingles tearing through me yet again.

'How do I look?' I ask, smoothing down my sleeveless T-shirt.

Only then do I remember that I haven't had a shower, or brushed my hair, or even cleaned my teeth. I rushed out of my house in such a hurry, thinking I could pop to the pharmacy and back in a matter of minutes. And the shorts I'm wearing aren't meant to be worn anywhere other than in my garden. I'd thrown them on to save time looking for anything else.

'Beautiful,' he says. 'But you always do.'

He coughs and abruptly sits upright, rubbing his fingers over the stubble on his chin.

I smile. It's as if he is thinking the same as I was just now. Had he popped out to the store, without a shower or a shave? His T-shirt is creased and his jeans have seen better days. He still looks devastatingly handsome; maybe even more so because he is dishevelled.

'Oh! You said you wanted a word, didn't you? In the pharmacy. I asked if you were in the queue and you said you weren't.'

He nods. 'Yes. I know. Erm. It can wait. You've got ten dates to get ready to meet. And although you look incredibly beautiful and sexy, I'm guessing you want to go home and get changed.'

Heat rushes to my face and it's not due to the rash.

I laugh nervously, wondering if he means any of that, hoping he does, wishing he would just take me in his arms and kiss me. But he won't. I'm pretty sure of that.

'You're right. I haven't even had a shower!'

He sniffs the air and pulls a face. 'I thought Nonna's healing potion never used to smell that bad.' And then he laughs, but there's sadness in his eyes. Is he remembering his grandmother? They were very close. Before he went away.

'Do you have a mirror?' I ask.

He nods towards the wall behind me. 'If you're going to ask it who the prettiest is, there's no need. I can tell you. It's me.' He winks at me.

'I can't argue with that,' I say, and something flashes across his eyes, but then I see my reflection and I'm amazed. 'Oh my God, Gio!'

My face is still redder than it should be, but it looks so much calmer. Gone are the angry raised spots, the blotches, and the lines. Now I look more like a smooth-skinned cherry, rather than an angry red planet.

'You're the one who should be making and selling skin care products, not Nuala.'

He smiles. 'I prefer to make and sell ice cream.'

'You've literally saved my day. I don't know how to thank you.'

His brows furrow momentarily but then he looks me in the eye and there's something akin to a challenge in his.

'No thanks needed, but if you feel you must, I'm sure you can think of something.'

'I must. I still owe you that espresso and bombolini.'

'Perhaps you can fit me in this weekend. If you have time between your dates.'

'Oh. Of course. I'm meeting them all on this pier, so we'll definitely do that this weekend.'

'I'm honoured.'

He doesn't sound it. He sounds annoyed now.

'I didn't mean it like that, Gio. I didn't mean I'd squeeze you in between all the other men.' Judging by the expression on his face, I'm making things worse. 'What I meant was, I'll be here most of this weekend and no matter what, I'm going to make sure I repay you for the ice cream. And now for your magic potion.'

'It was Nonna's potion, not mine. And there's nothing magic about it. Just fresh ingredients and herbs.'

'Gio? Have I said something to annoy

you? Because the last thing I meant to do was that. Although I did the same to Nuala yesterday, hence the need for the ice cream. But please tell me if I have.'

He studies my face for a few seconds and then he smiles. 'Don't worry. It's fine.' I follow him out and when we reach the door at the rear of La Dolce Vita, he adds, 'Oh, but about that magic potion. Make sure you're home in bed, alone, and before midnight, or you never know what might happen.'

'I'll be home alone in bed long before midnight. All my dates are during the day. Katie, Nan, and I decided it was better to meet them all in daylight.'

He grins. 'So you could weed out any vampires?'

'Possibly.' I laugh. 'But mainly because daylight feels safer. I know it doesn't get dark until late throughout the summer but an evening date feels more like a real date, whereas a date during the day is more like making new friends.'

He nods his head. 'I get that. And you're right. Now you'd better go, or you'll be late. And didn't you tell me, outside Alberto's the other day, that you are never, ever late?'

Thirteen

My emotions are in turmoil as I race along the pier. One minute Gio seems to be flirting with me and sending me signals that he's interested, the next, he's teasing me and telling me what to do, just like he did when I was that besotted, teenaged girl. Although, I think there's a very good chance I may still be besotted.

I call Nuala, on my drive home, and tell her about Gio's remedy, and I send her a photo of my face. She demands I introduce them, but she's laughing as she says it.

'I will do anything for that recipe,' she says. 'And I do mean, anything.'

'I don't think he'll divulge it because it's his Nonna's recipe.'

'I could ask her for it. Is she in Norman Landing?'

'She is. But you'd need a spiritualist to ask her. She died fourteen years ago. She's buried in cemetery of Holy Trinity Church.'

'Bugger. Okay. I'll have to work on Gio then.'

'Good luck with that. I know from personal experience that man can be as stubborn as a mule. And he keeps things close to his chest. Once he decides something, no torture on earth will get him to change his mind. Believe me. I know.'

'Hmm. It sounds as if you haven't told me and Mo everything about this Giovanni Russo. Okay. I'm gonna ask you outright and I want you to tell me the truth. Did you have sex with him? Emma? Did you hear me? I asked if you had sex with him?'

'I was fifteen when he left.'

'So? That doesn't answer my question.'

'No. It doesn't. The answer is, no. I didn't have sex with him. But I wanted to. I really, really wanted to.'

She shrieks with excitement. 'Tell me more. Tell me everything.'

'I am not discussing this over the phone, Nuala. Besides, I'm trying very hard not to think about Gio in the same sentence as the word 'sex', especially as I'm meeting ten different men this weekend. I need to keep my emotions and my hormones under control or God knows what might happen.'

'Losing control might do you good. Perhaps that's exactly what you need. A weekend of pure abandon. A weekend of nothing but sex.'

'With whom? I know, as a nurse for the NHS, you will not be condoning me having sex with ten different men.' I laugh.

'Maybe not ten, no, but one or two is okay. One today and one tomorrow. And as long as it's safe sex, that's fine.'

'Really? I'm not sure I could do that. Anyway, although Gio's remedy has worked miracles, my face is still a rather unbecoming shade of red. I'm not sure anyone would want to have sex with me.'

'Don't be stupid. They're men.'

'Point taken. I'll keep you informed.'

'You'd better. Mo and I are still considering paying La Dolce Vita a visit this weekend. Would it be weird if we did that, and you were there with one of your dates? We could pretend we don't know you.'

'Yes it would. Can't you wait until next weekend?'

She sighs. 'I suppose so. Will you call Mo to tell her about your miracle cure, or shall I?'

'Could you, please? I've got to call Katie and Nan and I'm almost home. I need to shower and get ready for my dates. Tell her I'll call her later.'

'Okay. I'll let her know the emergency is over and we can all stand down. Bye babe. Have fun!'

Her parting words remind me of Ben and I suddenly hear his voice telling me we've gone from DEFCON 1 to DEFCON 4. I wonder what he's doing. I bet he's having fun. I bet he's having plenty of sex, too.

I'm not sure why Ben having sex bothers me right now, or why he has popped into my head, when I've been fantasising all morning about having sex with Gio, but now that he has, I can't help but wonder how he would've reacted if he'd seen my face before Gio's remedy had worked its magic. Would he have told me I was beautiful, as Gio had? Hopefully, all signs of this rash will be gone by the time I see Ben again, so I'll probably never know.

Katie and Nan are as thrilled as I am that someone was able to help me with the rash, but neither one is quite as thrilled when I tell them it was Gio.

'Gio?' Katie says. 'Giovanni Russo?' As if there is another Gio. 'Wow! That's a surprise.'

Nan says something similar, although she adds, 'It's kind of him to help, sweetheart, and of course, he was in the right place at the right time, but is it wise to encourage his friendship? Everyone deserves a second chance, I know, and I wholeheartedly agree with that, but do people really change? I'm not convinced they do.'

'He doesn't need to change, Nan. He's not the man you think he is. He's kind and caring, and he's loyal and he's ... brave.'

'Your mother forbade you and Katie from seeing him, Emma, and you know she had a good reason. He stole. He lied on more than one occasion. Even his poor grandmother washed her hands of him. Don't forget that. My darling daughter would turn in her grave if she thought you and that Russo boy were...' She gasps as if she has just realised what she is saying. 'Oh my goodness. I am so sorry, sweetheart. I would never try to make you feel guilty. Or to feel that you were letting your mum down. She loved you more than life itself, as do I, and all that mattered to her, and to me, is that you and Katie are safe and happy and loved. Her own taste in men left a lot to be desired. We all agree on that. She would want you to find a man who truly loves you, Emma. A man like Katie's Aaron. Or my Donald. Or Tori's Mack. Well, you get the point. I don't think I need to labour it.'

'No Nan. You don't. But there's something I should tell you. And I should've said it long ago. When Mum was still alive.'

'Sorry, sweetheart. What was that? The phone signal seems to be cutting–' The line goes dead.

It is probably just as well. Confessions are better when made face to face, not over the phone. And Katie needs to hear it too. And possibly Aaron and Donald. And maybe, everyone, in truth. Perhaps it's time to set the record straight. Especially if Gio plans to stay in Norman Landing.

Fourteen

I decide to leave my long, dark brown hair loose and, as it's hot again today and a little humid I wear a sundress with narrow straps. The hem is short but not too short and it's low cut at the front, but again, not too low. The back is open to just above my waist. I want to look sexy and attractive, but I don't want these men to see every ounce of flesh. The dress is red with yellow maidenhair leaves scattered over it. Red may not have been a wise decision now that my face is a similar colour, but after I apply concealer and foundation, I'm delighted to see that my complexion is almost normal. It merely looks as if I've caught the sun.

I wear flat sandals for now as I'll be walking to the pier and then possibly on my feet for a lot of the day. I slip a pair of strappy, high heel sandals into a bag and add the skin care gifts I bought for Gio. I'll pop in to see him before I meet my first date so that I can give him the little gifts and, at the same time, ask if there is any chance I can leave my flatties in that cosy little room. I'm fairly sure he'll let me.

Katie pops round, along with Nan shortly before I leave, and they both give me a thumbs up. They can't believe how good my skin looks now compared to the way it looked earlier, so that gives me hope.

I'm nervous as I make my way to the pier but I'm also excited. It's been so long since I had a date and now, this weekend, I have ten! I still can't quite believe it. What happens if I like them all? What happens if they don't like me? What happens if they stand me up?

I tell myself not to worry about any of that right now and by the time I enter La Dolce Vita, I'm feeling very happy.

Until I see Gio. He's standing beside the gelato display cabinet with one arm resting on the top and his hand hanging over the edge. The other arm is bent in the air, an empty ice cream scoop in his hand, and he's laughing. Really laughing. As if he's genuinely happy.

The look in his eyes tells me that he likes what he sees – but what he sees is not me ... or the gelato; it's a tall, stunning brunette who must have just stepped out of a TV advert for an eye-wateringly expensive perfume. She has the perfect body and the longest, shapeliest, tanned legs I've ever seen. She's wearing the tightest, shortest, sexiest red dress that, unlike mine, leaves little to the imagination, and yet promises much more than you can see. She sways her hips seductively but so naturally and even I'm mesmerised by her as she moves from one foot to the other on the highest heels ever made. She flicks a lock of her glossy mane of waist-length, brunette hair over her bare shoulder and laughs, and it's as sexy and seductive as the woman herself, and when she speaks, her voice is like the rest of her: perfect in every way. It's warm and friendly, sexy and seductive, mysterious and full of promise.

And that's when it dawns on me that I've seen this woman before. And not that long ago. Just a matter of weeks, in fact. Unless I am very much mistaken. Which, I suppose, I could be. My Ben looks exactly like the actor, Ben, and even has the same name. Leo looks exactly like my Ben, so this woman, who has her back to me, might be someone else who just happens to look and sound like the woman I think it may be. I'll wait until I see her face.

'Oh, Gio,' she coos. 'You are teasing me. How can I possibly choose when everything looks so tempting? So delicious. So ... naughty, but oh so nice. I need you to decide.

I am in your hands. I know you will give me whatever you feel I would enjoy. But don't make me wait too long. I am hot and I am hungry. And not just for ice cream, Gio. As I said, *everything* here is *soooo* tempting. And I have never been able to resist temptation.'

I want to fade into the background. But then I realise I already have. No one in La Dolce Vita has eyes or ears for anyone or anything other than this amazing goddess. This dark-haired Venus. This paragon. This Siren.

I'm hoping that, by some miracle, she's ugly, but if she's who I think she is, she is the opposite of ugly. She's the epitome of perfection.

When, to my amazement, Gio spots me and says my name as if he's pleased to see me, the woman turns and looks at me, with eyes like sapphires and a smile on her full, bright red, cherubic lips and I am not mistaken. It is her. Or her double.

This is Geneva McBriar. Mack Fisher's former, 'fake' fiancée. Tori's boyfriend's ex. The most beautiful woman on the planet. And apparently one of the richest.

Life definitely isn't fair. How can one woman have all that?

And yet ... she doesn't have Mack. He chose Tori over her. And despite being with Geneva for around five years, he told us all he never loved her. We all believe him. So perhaps being beautiful and wealthy doesn't make life any easier where love is concerned. There's an odd sort of comfort in that.

I wonder what she's doing back in Norman Landing? Does Mack know she's here? Or Tori? Is Geneva still hoping to buy Seascape Café? Has no one told her that ship has sailed? Or is she still interested in Conqueror's Court? Is she competing with Trulove Hotels for that property? I thought that was as good as done and dusted. Or is there another reason she's here? Surely she's not hoping she might get Mack back? That will never happen, if I know Mack at all.

'I'm so sorry,' she says to me. 'I simply can't decide. I may be here for some time.' She clearly has no idea who I am or that I know who she is. But then why would she? She only had eyes for Mack and for Tori that day. And then she turns back to Gio. 'I hope that isn't a problem. I'm sure a man like you has better ways of spending his time than waiting for a woman like me to select which flavour of ice cream she wants to lick. Perhaps we should let your other customers go first. As long as you don't mind me being here until I make my pick.'

'Nope,' he says. 'We're open all day and we don't close until midnight. You've got plenty of time.' And then he pushes himself away from the display case, places the scoop back in its stand, says, 'Excuse me,' to Geneva, and comes and stands in front of me. 'Here for more ice cream? Or for secret family remedies?'

I beam at him as I bask in the warmth of his smile.

'Neither. I'm here to give you a gift. And to ask a favour.'

A crease appears between his brows but there's an amused expression on his face.

'That sounds a lot like bribery. What's the favour?'

'Don't you want the gift first?'

'Nope. I might feel obliged to grant the favour once I've seen the gift. This way I won't feel guilty if I refuse.'

'I wondered if I could leave my flat shoes here, in that room we were in earlier, perhaps? I'm wearing these while I'm on my dates.' I pull my high heeled sandals from my bag and dangle them in front of him. 'If I have to stand in these all day I'll be crippled and I'll have to ask you to carry me home. Or call me a cab, at least. I'll come back later and change back into my flats. Would that be okay?'

He grins at me. 'I should think so. But I'm happy to carry you home if you need me to.' He holds out his hand and I place mine in his for balance while I change into my high heels. He's laughing and I'm not sure why, but I notice Geneva is staring at me. And she doesn't look pleased.

'What's so funny?' I ask him in a low voice so that she can't hear.

He's still sniggering as he leans forward and whispers, 'You are, Emma. In a good way. I was holding my hand out for my gift. But hey. Feel free to use me in any way you want.' His eyes meet mine and the look that passes between us sends my heart fluttering towards the ceiling.

'Oh. I'm sorry.'

'Don't be. I like holding your hand.' My heart flutters higher.

'Erm. Here's your gift. It's skin care products from last night.'

I hand him the bag and now his brows knit tightly together.

'The same skin care products that brought you out in a rash? Thanks. That's exceedingly kind.'

'I got them last night before I saw the rash. And I'm the only one who was allergic, so it's because there's something wrong with me, not the products.'

'There's nothing wrong with you, Emma.' He grins suddenly. 'Nothing that I don't have a magic cure for, anyway. So you think my skin needs some care?' He pulls out one of the products, unscrews the lid and smells it. 'It smells good.'

'I think your skin is perfect as it is. But we all like a bit of pampering now and then, don't we? Even men.'

'Oh yes. This man likes a lot of pampering. Are you going to show me how to apply this?' His eyes dance with devilment.

'There are instructions on the bottle.'

'Spoilsport.'

'Excuse me.' Geneva has come to join us. 'I wasn't eavesdropping. Honestly. But are those homemade skincare products? Only you must be extremely careful with those. Not all the products come from legitimate sources, and some contain all types of nasties. A friend of mine has been left with permanent scarring. And another's face was red and blotchy for days and days.' She looks me directly in the eye. 'Have you been using them?'

My hand instinctively flies to my face. Have the blotches returned?

Gio reads my mind and glares at Geneva but then he smiles at me.

'No sign of any blotches, Emma. You look beautiful. Don't worry.'

'Are you sure?'

He nods. 'Absolutely.'

'You look lovely,' Geneva says. 'I didn't mean to imply otherwise. I'm sorry if you misunderstood. I just wanted to warn you.'

Her tone is so warm and caring that I almost believe her. Almost. But I know who she is and there's a hint of ice in her eyes when she looks at me which disappears when she turns her gaze to Gio.

'I think I know exactly what I want now, Gio.'

'So do I,' he says, looking directly at me.

The bells of the clock on the tower of Holy Trinity Church ring out the hour and I gasp as I hear the distant sound. 'I'm late for my first date!' I shove my sandals at Gio and he takes them, then I hurry out of La Dolce Vita, saying, 'I can't be late. I'll see you later.'

'Have fun,' he calls after me. 'But not too much.'

Fifteen

Who knew dating could be so exhausting? Or so boring? Or so annoying? Certainly not me. But then it's been ages since I've had a date.

My first date of the day is with Paul. He looks exactly like his photo, so that's a good start. Unfortunately that is the only thing that is good about him.

Despite me being on time, as I only had a few feet to cover from La Dolce Vita to where we had agreed to meet at the end of the pier, Paul is fifteen minutes late. I'm about to give up on him when he saunters into view, seemingly untroubled by his tardiness.

In his photo, his mouth is closed as he smiles. Now his mouth is open – and he's got two gold teeth right at the front of his mouth!

I hope I'm not a judgemental person when it comes to looks and to personal taste, but there is no way I can date a man who has two gold front teeth. I can't drag my gaze from them. I hate myself for that but it's true. It's a bit like when a man stares at a woman's breasts while the woman is speaking. I'm staring at Paul's teeth and I simply can't stop myself.

'You must be E,' he says. 'You looked prettier in your photo.'

Poor time management and poor manners score against him, and what's with this 'E' business?

'I'm Emma, yes. Was the traffic bad?'

'Traffic? No. It was fine. I came by bus. Stopped off at a couple of pubs on the way.'

'I see.' I'm not sure I do, but I can't be bothered seeking clarity.

We walk around the circular section of the pier for a few minutes and we'll be passing La Dolce Vita any second. I can't help wishing I was there instead of here with Paul.

'You haven't mentioned my teeth,' he says. 'Had them done in Poland.' He stops and tugs at his lips to provide me with a better view. 'They're great aren't they? Much cheaper out there.'

I think that's what he said. He's still holding his lips so it's a bit difficult to discern exactly what he's saying.

'They're certainly ... gold.'

'Yep. Having more done when I've got the cash. Some people have tattoos. I have gold teeth.'

He's now let go of his lips so that part of his conversation is clear. I'm not a fan of tattoos either, but they are preferable to gold teeth. I think.

'My mum loves them. Tatts, as we call them, not gold teeth. But she does like my teeth.' He smiles, and I wish he wouldn't. 'She's covered in tatts. Even her toes.' He leans close and nudges my arm. 'And her private bits. She might show them to you if you ask. Lots of people wanna see them. She's famous on some websites.'

Okay. I've had enough. I know I don't want to date Paul, and I have no wish to see any of his mother's tatts, or anything else come to that.

'That's so interesting, Paul. But my phone is vibrating and I'm expecting an important call. I hope you don't mind if I take it.'

'Vibrating phone, eh? Is that what you women call them these days?'

I don't even want to know what he's referring to. I turn away and pretend to answer a call.

'Oh no! Surely not. Of course. I'll be right there.' I pretend to ring off and I smile apologetically. 'I am so, so sorry, Paul, but my friend, Gio, needs me. I'm afraid I must leave. It was lovely to meet you.'

'Can I get your number? We'll make

another date.'

'I'm sorry, but I don't give out my number, and I'm not sure we're a fit. I've also recently discovered I have some allergies. I think gold may be one of them. I wish you luck for your next date. Goodbye.'

I can't really walk in my high heels but somehow I manage to run. I suppose that must be my survival instinct kicking in.

I dash into La Dolce Vita and hide behind a large cardboard Knickerbocker Glory.

'No licking of the cardboard ice cream sundaes,' Gio says, a few moments later. 'Aren't you meant to be on a date?'

He laughs hysterically when I tell him about Paul. I notice Geneva isn't around.

'Did Geneva leave here satisfied?'

'Geneva? Oh, that woman.' He shrugs. 'I think so. She said she'll definitely be back, so I assume she was happy.'

I proceed to tell him who she is and how I know her.

'Lucky Mack,' he says.

'Yes. She's gorgeous I must admit, and he did date her for about five years.'

His brow creases. 'No. I meant lucky escape.'

'What? Are you telling me you wouldn't want to date her?'

He nods. 'Yes. A woman like that is only

interested in one thing.'

'Sex, you mean? Surely that's a positive for most men?'

He shakes his head. 'Herself. She's only interested in her own happiness. She's good to look at, I'll agree, but to date? No thanks. I prefer my dates to at least be vaguely interested in me as well as themselves.'

'I do think she was genuinely interested in Mack. But I may be wrong. Are ... are you dating anyone now?'

He grins at me.

'No. Although there's a dating site I'm considering joining, so who knows.'

'Really? You ... you're going to look for some women to date?'

He shrugs. 'We'll see. I'd only be looking for one special woman.'

I sigh wistfully. 'I think that's what we're all looking for. That one special person to share our lives with.'

'But some of us aren't looking in the right place.'

He sounds annoyed again as he marches away to serve some customers but I can't think what I've said to upset him.

I go outside to the end of the pier to sit in the sunshine and wait for my next date.

I don't have long to wait. Jake is thirty minutes early. I'm on a call with Mo when he arrives. Again, he looks like his photo, and when he smiles, his teeth are white and straight and healthy-looking. As is he. He's smaller than his profile states, closer to five-feet-five than six-feet-three, and in my heels, I tower over him as I stand to greet him.

'Bloody hell, it's hot,' he says. 'What made you choose this place? I could murder a cold beer.'

'La Dolce Vita serves beer.'

'Does it have a TV?'

'N-no.'

He glances at his watch and curses again. 'Okay. Shall we go somewhere else?'

'To watch TV? I don't think so. But please don't let me stop you.'

He looks me up and down – twice, smiles, waves a hand in the air, and says, 'Later,' as he hurries away.

Clearly TV is far more appealing than me.

'I think I've inherited Mum's taste in men,' I tell Katie when I call her five minutes later.

'Were they really that bad?' She's trying hard not to let me hear her laughing, I can tell.

'Yes. Shall I simply cancel the rest? An upset tummy seems preferable right now.'

'Third time lucky,' she says. 'The next one is Tim, isn't it? The doctor.'

'Yes. But the way my luck is going he's

probably a doctor of the university of life, and not a real doctor at all.'

'You've got ten dates, Emma. They won't all be bad. The law of averages dictates that at least some of them will be nice.'

And Katie is right. Tim is nice. Plus, he's a real doctor. A General Practitioner in a large practice in Brighton.

He's tall, broad-shouldered, and handsome. He has a lovely smile with perfect teeth. His mother is in the W.I. and doesn't like tattoos, and his father is a vicar.

Tim cycles, runs, and plays tennis. He loves to swim, and takes long walks. He doesn't have any pets but would be open to having one. He doesn't mind what. Cat, dog, or anything really. He seems quite easy going.

'But that's enough about me,' he says with a lovely smile. 'Tell me more about you.'

I reel off my life story, or at least the interesting parts of it, which doesn't take very long. I tell him Dad left us, and how and when Mum died.

He reaches out and touches my hand as we walk. 'I'm so sorry for your loss,' he says. 'SADS is always horrendous for those left behind. They want answers and we don't have them. I know it's no consolation but at least your mum died quickly and wasn't in any pain.'

'That's the only comfort. Knowing Mum didn't suffer. But I still miss her dreadfully, especially at times like this.'

'Times like this?' His strong brows knit together.

'When I'm going on dates.'

'Dates? As in several?'

'Erm. Yes. I've actually got a few dates this weekend. Is ... is that a problem?'

He coughs. 'No.'

'Surely you've arranged to see other people?'

'I haven't. As I believe I mentioned, I'm new to online dating. One of the receptionists at our practice suggested it, and to be honest, I was sceptical. Until I saw your profile. I liked the look of you right away. This probably sounds old fashioned, but I don't believe in open relationships in any way, shape, or form. I know we're not *in* a relationship but I wanted to start off the way I mean to go on, seeing one person at a time. If this date comes to nothing, I'll try again. Does that sound weird?'

'No. I think that's lovely. It makes a refreshing change to hear a man say he only wants to date one woman at a time.'

He smiles. 'Phew. That's a relief. It's going well so far, isn't it?'

'Yes. I think it is.'

We find we have other things in

common. We both like good wine and delicious food, but then again, so do most people. We both love Star Trek movies, but not so much that we go to any conventions. We both love to see different places and meet new people. And we both love pottering in the garden. He has his own house in Brighton. He hopes to have children one day. Two would be good, three even better. I like the sound of that. And we've already discussed the possibility of having a pet.

I can't believe it's 1.30 and we met at noon. The time has flown.

'I'd love to see you again, Emma,' he says when I tell him I've arranged to meet my best friends for lunch.

'I'd love to see you too. But you do understand about my other dates, don't you?'

He nods. 'I do. I like to think I'm a reasonable man, so we'll say no more about it. Hopefully, by our second date, you'll have whittled it down to just me.' He smiles. 'I'm joking. But maybe by our third date?'

I like him, but I'm not prepared to make any promises or commitments.

'Maybe. We'll see.'

Something flashes across his eyes but it's gone in seconds and the lovely smile returns.

'I'll say goodbye until next time then. Are you free on Monday evening?'

139

'Oh. Erm.' That's a bit quick, but at least he's keen. 'This week is difficult because a work colleague is away all week and I'm covering his team as well as mine. What about next weekend?'

'Next weekend is good. Saturday? Same time? Would you like to come to Brighton? Or I'm happy to come back here.'

'Why don't we have a think and message one another with suggestions, via the dating site? I'm sure you'll understand I don't want to give out my phone number on a first date.'

'Of course. There are some oddballs around. Better to stay safe. I'll message you. May I kiss you on the cheek? Or is it too soon?'

'The cheek is fine.'

He leans forward, puts his hand on my arm, and gives me a peck on my cheek. I can feel the pressure of his fingers and when he releases me, I'm not entirely surprised to see thin red marks. But I know he was nervous and he probably didn't realise his grip was so tight.

Katie and Nan are meeting me for lunch at Seascape Café but I didn't want to tell Tim it was my sister and my nan. I'm not sure why I lied. It just seemed easier to say I was meeting my best friends.

Gio is busy with customers when I return to La Dolce Vita to collect my flatties so I nip into the back room, change my shoes, and leave him a note.

'Date number two was as bad as number one, but number three is promising and he's keen to see me again. He's a GP, his mum's in the W.I. and his dad's a vicar. A match made in heaven? I've changed my shoes and I'm meeting Katie and Nan for lunch but I'll see you later. I've got two more dates this afternoon, but would love to buy you that espresso and bombolini later this afternoon, if you have time. Leave me a message here.'

I draw a big arrow beneath my last sentence, pointing down to a delineated box with the words, 'Yes please, Emma. I would love to join you for coffee and doughnuts at … (please fill in the time, here)' I hope he finds it amusing.

I hurry along Beachland Road and I have the strangest feeling I'm being followed, which I know is utterly ludicrous, but shivers run up and down my spine as if someone has walked over my grave.

Katie and Nan are waiting at the table Tori has reserved for us on the wooden deck of Seascape Café.

'I'm not late, am I?' I glance at my watch as I rush towards them, and again I get that creepy feeling but as I spin round to look behind me, I bump into Tori. 'Sorry!'

'I'll live,' she says. 'You look worried.

What's up? Were your dates all zombies and now they're following you?'

I laugh. 'You don't know how close to the truth that is.'

Tori links her arm through mine and we join Katie and Nan at the table. The sandy beach below is heaving with tourists, as is the deck of the café, along with the tables and chairs inside. The tide is out and the bluest sea I've seen for a long time melds into the almost matching, cloudless sky.

Tori sighs as she sits down. 'I've been on my feet since 6.00 a.m. and I'm exhausted but I've never felt this happy in my life. I just wish I had another partner who was willing to work hard, knows how to run a restaurant and deal with a few difficult customers, and also knows how to have a laugh. Know anyone like that?'

She's looking pointedly at Katie, who grins. 'I think Donald's looking for a part time job.'

'Get away with you,' says Nan. 'He's got plenty to occupy him in our new home.'

Katie sighs. 'I have been thinking about it, Tori. Honestly I have. And I think...' She grins mischievously. 'When do you want me to start?'

Tori leaps up, almost knocking the tray of cocktails that Mack is bringing us, out of his hands.

'We need champagne!' says Tori. 'Katie's going to join us in our business.'

'That's wonderful news,' Mack says, setting the tray on the table, and everyone hugs one another.

'You can start as soon as you like,' Tori informs Katie. 'Or if you need more time while Silvio and Alberto find a replacement, that's fine too. Whenever. I don't mind. I'm just so happy you'll be here soon.'

Katie smiles. 'I've already discussed it with Silvio and Alberto, because after you told me you'd like me to be involved, I felt sort of guilty not telling them. I knew they'd be fine about it. They're both such lovely people. They said they'll be sorry to see me leave, but they know this will mean a better future for me, and they have always wanted what was best for anyone who has ever worked for them. I'd like to stay on for another week or so, if that's okay. They've got some new staff starting and I said I'd help train them up. After everything they've done for me I want to do something in return.'

'Of course. No problem at all. Start whenever you want.'

Tori dashes off to get champagne while Mack serves other customers.

'You were right about third time lucky,' I say to Katie as we sit down, and I tell her and Nan about Tim.

'He sounds nice,' says Nan, but I can tell she's hesitant.

'What's wrong?'

She glances at Katie. 'Nothing. Except, perhaps ... he does sound a little ... possessive.'

'Possessive? How?'

'The bit about only dating one person at a time.'

'That's lovely. I'd rather that than the alternative.'

'But this was your first date. Maybe on the third or fourth, he could mention that he'd like you both to be exclusive, but on a first date? No.'

'I don't know,' says Katie. 'If he really likes her, what's wrong with wanting her to see just him?'

Nan shrugs. 'I may be wrong. But it would be a potential red flag for me.'

When Tori and Mack return, I ask what they think.

'Red flag,' says Tori.

'He must like you a lot if he's already jealous,' says Mack. 'But on the whole, I think I agree with Tori.'

'But ... he seems so perfect ... in almost every way.'

'They always do, sweetheart,' Nan says. 'That doesn't mean you shouldn't see him again. It might've been nerves, or that he doesn't know how dating sites work, as he said. Just don't go to Brighton. Make him come here. And one of us will be close by, just in case.'

'I thought dating was supposed to be fun!' I say, as Tori pops the cork of the champagne.

Sixteen

Gio is nowhere to be seen when I go to change my shoes, but La Dolce Vita is as packed as Seascape Café had been, so he must be somewhere. I glance at the note, and to my delight he's written the words, 'Anytime. Your wish is my command', and then he's drawn another arrow, that leads to another piece of paper on his desk, and then another and another until I'm following a trail of sheets of paper and arrows. They lead to a heavy door and I knock and call out his name.

'Hello,' he says, opening the door to reveal a large cold-room.

'Hello,' I reply. 'Why are you hiding in the fridge?'

He grins. 'I'm working. I'm doing a quick stock-take. If we continue to be as busy as this, I'll run out of a few things within a matter of days.'

'A likely story. You're just avoiding the

heat and the customers, aren't you?'

'You're right. So date number three was good?'

'He was.'

'But? There is a but, isn't there?'

'There wasn't. Until I met Katie and the others. Ooh! Katie is going to join Tori and Mack at Seascape Café! And Lou and Dave, of course, but they're semi-retired now and Mack will be starting his new job, so it'll just be Tori and Katie running the place. Oh damn it! I didn't tell them about Geneva.'

'I think we've gone off on a bit of a tangent here. You were telling me about your third date's but.' He grins. 'As in, "Houston we have a problem".'

That makes me laugh. 'But ... they all think he might be a tad possessive.'

Gio tenses. 'Possessive? Why?'

I tell him exactly what happened on the date.

'Wow. It sounds as if you're about to book the church. No doubt his dad will perform the ceremony.'

'We've only just met, Gio.'

'It only takes a moment to fall in love.'

'I'm not in love! I like him and I'd like to get to know him better, but I'm not about to buy a wedding dress.'

'I'm glad to hear it. I agree with everyone else. If a man tells you on your first date that he doesn't want you to see other men, that's a little worrying.'

'So, if you were in his shoes, you wouldn't care about me seeing other men?'

He gives me an odd look. 'There's a difference between caring and controlling. A big difference. Do I care? Yes. Am I happy about it? No. Will I try to stop you? Absolutely not. It's your life. You must decide who and what you want.'

He darts a look at me as if he's said more than he meant to and I suddenly realise exactly what he has said.

'Gio?'

'No!' He looks me directly in the eye. 'Your mum forbade you from seeing me.'

I nod in both amazement and disbelief. 'I know. But I did. And ... we're friends now, aren't we?'

'Yes. Friends.'

'But ... are you wondering if–'

'No. Your sister and your Nan have a very low opinion of me.'

'Yes, but that's only because–'

'It would never work, Emma.' He sighs. 'One minute I think it could, the next I realise it can't. Too many people know about the past.'

'But they don't know what–'

'It doesn't matter. And if you think for one minute that either of us can tell the truth now, after all these years, you're wrong.'

'Will you stop interrupting me! I let you take the blame for something I did. I should never have done that.'

'It was my choice. I insisted.'

'You were wrong then, and I think you're wrong now. You paid a price you should never have paid. You had to leave here because of me. Because of what I did. You let your nan believe you were a thief and a liar. I know how much she meant to you. I know that broke your heart. And for what? For a stupid fifteen-year-old girl who should've known better. And should've been brave enough to take the blame for what she did.'

'I wouldn't let you. So it wasn't your fault. And it could've been worse. I could've gone to prison. But I didn't. The money was repaid. Charges were never filed. All I had to do was leave here. Leave my family and leave you. I thought it would be easy. I'll admit I was wrong about that.'

'It's time, Gio. It's time it all came out.'

He shakes his head. 'No. Best to let sleeping dogs lie. Now I think it's time you went on your next date. We'll pretend this conversation didn't happen. We'll never speak of this again. Just as we agreed fifteen years ago.'

'We didn't agree, Gio. You insisted. And I was too scared and too foolish to do what I should've done. You've just said there's a big difference between caring and controlling. I know you did what you did because you cared. But in a way, you took control away from me. And I need to take that back.'

He shakes his head again. 'Don't do this, Emma. Promise me.'

'I've got to do what's right.'

'Why? Raking up old mud doesn't always clear the path, sometimes all it does is transfer that mud elsewhere. You've got a great career, a fantastic family, you're happy, and now you're going for what you want in the world of dating. I've had a good life, despite the way I left. Now I'm back and I own La Dolce Vita. I've got a fresh start.'

'You own this place? I had no idea. I thought Alberto owned it.'

He smirks. 'A natural assumption, given our history. But no. It's me. He and Silvio handled things until I could finalise the sale of my business in the States.'

'That's where you've been all these years? I had heard you went there, but no one ever talked about you after you left and ... I was too scared to ask anyone for news.'

'I didn't intend to return, but I did keep in touch with Alberto and when the opportunity came up to open this place, he told me about it right away. I don't want to lose it, Emma. I don't want to open old wounds.' He stares at me and I can see the heartbreak in his eyes.

'But surely you want people to know the truth, don't you? Everyone, including Katie and Nan would see you as the saviour you are instead of the devil they believe you to be.'

'And how would they see you? I know Katie and Nan would still love you, but what about all the others who hear of it?'

'I ... I don't care what people think of me.'

'You do, Emma. And rightly so. And I care too. If you are determined to do this, there's nothing more for us to say. But I'm begging you to think about it. Really think about it. You think you'd be doing both of us a favour by setting the record straight. You wouldn't. All it would do is make my leaving here all those years ago, a total waste of time.'

'But I ...' I'm so confused I don't know what to say.

Gio says, 'Please close the door on your way out.' And he turns his back on me.

Seventeen

I was so happy when I walked into the cold-room. Now I feel like ice, in more ways than one. I'm fairly certain Gio has just told me he has feelings for me. Romantic feelings. And yet he's not intending to pursue them because of what happened in the past. But when I made it clear I want to set the record straight, instead of him being pleased, he was angry and hurt and looked at me as if he felt betrayed.

I don't know what to think. I don't know what to do. And the thought of meeting two more dates fills me with dread instead of excitement.

And what about my coffee date with Gio? Is that still on?

He said we should forget the conversation happened. But is that really possible?

He's right about my life. And from what he's just told me about his, perhaps he's right about the past. He now owns La Dolce Vita. He's got a fresh start. If I tell the truth now, it will all be raked up again, he's right about that. And he wasn't always innocent. That's how it all started. Perhaps I do need to think about this further. Maybe I should let sleeping dogs lie.

'Excuse me, but are you Emma?'

I'm miles away when I hear my fourth date's voice and for a moment I can't remember his name.

'Yes,' I say, forcing a smile. 'Sorry I was in a world of my own. It's lovely to meet you.' I don't recall his face either, although I can hardly see it above the huge bouquet of flowers he's holding.

'Then these are for you.' He hands me the bouquet, smiles, and walks away, adding, 'Have a lovely afternoon.'

What has just happened?

'Wait!' I hurry after him as fast as I can in my high heels. 'What about our date?'

He turns and gives me the strangest look.

'I think you have me confused with someone else. I'm from *Blooms in Time*, the florists on Sea Road.' He points to the badge he's wearing on his dark green polo shirt. 'May I suggest you read the card.' He smiles again and adds, 'Have a lovely afternoon.' That's the second time he's said that.

The card? I search for a card amongst the beautiful blooms and for one foolish moment I actually wonder if the flowers are from Gio. But he wouldn't have had time to order them, and besides, after our conversation, I don't think flowers are likely.

I spot the card and read the words.

'Beautiful flowers for a beautiful woman. I'm looking forward to our second date, and many more after that. See you very soon, Tim.'

Tim? Tim has sent me flowers? But how did he know where to find me?

I told him I had more dates, but did I say I was meeting all of them here? And how did he know what time to send them?

I put the bouquet on a bench that's just become vacant and sit beside them dialling the number on the card.

'*Blooms in Time.* Angie speaking. How may I help you?'

'Hi Angie. This is Emma. I have a strange question for you and I hope you can help. Someone from your shop has just given me a bouquet. It's from a man called Tim and it was delivered to me at the end of Norman Landing pier. I don't suppose you could tell me when it was ordered and what the delivery instructions were, could you? Only it was a bit of a surprise and it's made me feel a bit weird.'

'Blimey. I mean, I'll certainly see if I can help. Hold the line for just a second while I check our list of deliveries for today.'

She's humming in the background and then she says, 'Got it! Hello, Emma. Are you still there?'

'I'm here.'

'Okay. It was a walk-in. That means the person came into the shop. The bouquet was made to the customer's specification. He chose the flowers. The order was placed at 3.00 p.m. and he paid the super express delivery fee. We've got standard, express, and super express. Super express guarantees immediate delivery. Well, within half an hour to a local address. And the note says that your name is Emma, you'll be at the end of the pier and that you're five-feet-five, with long, dark brown hair and you're wearing a red sundress dotted with yellow maidenhair leaves. Blimey. We wouldn't usually accept an order like that. We normally require a specific address. I was on my lunch break so it wasn't me who took the order, and now Jean's on hers so I can't ask her anything else.'

'Thanks, Angie. That's really helpful.'

'Is there anything else I can help you with?'

'No thanks. You've been great.'

'Has that made you feel better or worse?'

'I'm not really sure.'

'Well, I hope you'll leave us a good review. Have a lovely afternoon.'

'You too.'

I ring Katie straight after. 'You will never believe this,' I say. 'Tim has sent me flowers.'

'Tim? The doctor? How?'

I tell her what Angie told me.

'That is creepy. If he placed the order at 3.00 that means he must've hung around. Your date ended at 1.30, didn't it?'

'It did. You know, I got the feeling I was being followed when I met you and Nan for lunch. Do you think he was following me and he saw me come back here and then went and ordered the flowers so that they'd arrive when I might be on another date?'

'I suppose it's possible. Creepy and weird, but possible. Is there a phone number or anything on the card?'

'Only the florists' number. And that message. Maybe he thinks he's being romantic.'

'No, Emma. He's being weird. I think perhaps you should ghost him.'

'I can't do that. Maybe I'll tell him I like someone else and I don't want a second date after all. Oooh. I've just spotted number four. I'll call you later.'

Number four is Tony, and he seems so normal and so nice that I'm actually relieved.

He's a few inches taller than me, is dressed casually in jeans and a T-shirt and has very neat hair. He jokes about the flowers. At least I think he's joking.

'I hope those aren't for me because I didn't get you anything,' he says, smiling. And it's a lovely smile.

I explain they're from an earlier date, and he doesn't bat an eyelid. He works in finance but he doesn't say as what. He has three sisters and a brother, two dogs, four cats and a rabbit. He's been married before but it didn't work out and they parted as friends. He's back at his mum's temporarily but is moving into another place of his own in two weeks, now that the marital home has sold. And, like me, he has several dates this weekend. We chat for a while but although I like him, I'm not getting any vibes and there's no chemistry between us.

'Great to meet you, Emma, but I don't see a future, do you? I'm looking for someone who's willing to give up work and run the home, feed the kids, walk the dogs, stuff like that.'

Okay, maybe not quite so normal after all.

Are there any normal guys on this damn dating site?

Date number five is a non-starter from the off. He waves a packet of sandwiches at me and then proceeds to open it and eat them. I have nothing against people who eat while walking, especially if they missed lunch and haven't eaten since breakfast, but I do have a problem with people talking with their mouths full. And when the sandwiches are tuna and sweetcorn, and little bullets of hard, yellow corn keep hitting me on the cheek, I definitely take exception. He doesn't even mention the flowers. It's as if he hasn't seen them. And he doesn't ask one thing about me, apart from whether I like tuna.'

I'm not saying today has been a complete waste of time, but if this is what the men on online dating sites are like, I think I may need an alternative method of finding my prince. All I've had today is a bunch of frogs.

And a bouquet of flowers from a possible stalker.

Eighteen

Gio must still be in the cold-room because there's no sign of him when I peer through the glass frontage. I make my way inside and am pleased the queue is short, but Abbie, one of Gio's staff, sees me and waves me to the front.

'Gio's in the back,' she says. 'You can go through if you want.'

'Actually, we're supposed to be having a coffee. Any chance of a table? Outside, preferably.' I smile apologetically at the man who was at the front of the queue. 'Sorry. Perks of knowing the owner.'

'No worries. Nice flowers.'

He smiles and something flutters in my stomach. Clearly Australian judging from the accent. The shoulder-length blond hair, naturally tanned and slightly weather-beaten skin, broad chest and smattering of blond chest-hairs beneath his open, colourful, short-sleeved shirt, and the knee-length khaki shorts he's wearing, along with flip-flops on his otherwise bare feet, suggest he's possibly a surfer.

'Table five is free,' says Abbie.

'Great. Erm. I don't suppose you could tell Gio to meet me outside, could you? Only we had a bit of a ... disagreement and I might get a frosty reception.'

'He's in the cold-room, so you'll get that anyway, but sure. I'll tell him.'

'Boyfriend trouble?' The Australian asks. 'Is that who the blooms are for?'

I shake my head. 'Friend trouble. These are from a potential boyfriend. But I'm crossing him off my list.'

'That raises so many questions. Don't you like the flowers? You have a list of potential boyfriends? Can anyone make the list? Are there any Aussies on it? If not, would you like one?'

I laugh. 'I love the flowers, it's the sentiment that concerns me. I've taken my first steps into online dating this weekend, so yes, there's a list. My sister and my nan are supposed to be vetting my dates, although the ones I'm seeing this weekend are mainly my choice. I have to question my taste, judging by the ones I've met so far. No Aussies, no. But yes. I'm open to any nationality. Do you live near here or are you just visiting?'

'Ah. Looking for 'The One', eh? That's a shame. I'm here for the summer and then it's back to Aus, so unless you're up for moving, I guess I won't make the list.'

'That *is* a shame,' I say.

'I've told him,' says Abbie, with a sigh. 'He wasn't happy, but he says he'll be there in a sec. Want coffee?'

'Cappuccino, please. And I'm paying for Gio's, and for two bombolini for him. And whatever this lovely man here is having. For letting me queue jump and for being so nice about it.'

He raises a hand. 'No need for that. Nice chat.'

'I want to. You've cheered me up.'

He smiles. 'Thanks. I hope you find what you're looking for. But if not, and you fancy a trip to Aus, look me up.' He hands me a card with a full-length picture of him holding a surfboard, standing in front of the ocean with massive waves rolling in behind him and it says, *Bill's Boards*, on the card. There's an address and phone number on it.

'Is this you?'

'Nah. Found it on the beach.' He laughs.

I grin. 'I meant, is this your business?'

'I know you did. And yep. That's me.'

'Hello, Bill. It's lovely to meet you. I'm Emma.'

'I'm John. Lovely to meet you too.'

161

'John?'

'Kidding.' He laughs again.

I give him a little wave and go and sit at table five. Abbie brings my coffee, an espresso and the bombolini, and as she's walking back inside, Gio strides towards me. He does a double take when he sees the flowers that are on the chair beside me but he takes the seat opposite me, in silence.

I sip my coffee and he sips his and then he takes a bite out of one of the Nutella-filled doughnuts. It's not the silence I mind. I'm happy to sit in silence with him at any time. It's the fact that he's evidently trying to ignore me that hurts.

'So we're not going to talk?' I ask.

He shrugs and munches his food.

'Oh come on, Gio. I'm sorry. Okay? I promise I'll think about everything you said and I'll talk to you about it again before I do anything.'

He nods and continues eating.

'Aren't you going to say anything? Anything at all?'

He swallows and frowns at me. 'I was eating. I don't speak with food in my mouth. But now I've finished, so I can.' He nods towards the chair. 'Nice flowers.'

'They're from Tim.'

'Tim? The possessive guy? Did he come back?'

I shake my head but just as I'm about to explain, Bill, the Australian strolls by, a take-away cup of coffee in his hand.

'Thanks again for the coffee, Emma. See you on the beach, maybe. Catch you later.'

'Yes. Maybe. Bye.'

'Another date?' Gio asks with a sigh.

'No. Actually I met him in the queue in La Dolce Vita.'

'In there?' He nods his head towards the building.

'Yeah. Nothing like that ever happens to me.'

'So you bought him coffee?'

'No. I bought him coffee because he let me jump the queue.'

Gio takes another bite of his doughnut, and this time it's a big one, so we sit in silence for some time.

Eventually he speaks again. 'How did the dates go this afternoon?'

'Not well.'

'Five more dates tomorrow?'

I nod. 'And I'm tired of it already. How do people do this?'

'Date?'

'Find a prince in a world full of frogs.'

'If you're looking for a prince, you're going to be disappointed. They're a rarity. Most of us are just ordinary guys, doing ordinary things.'

There is nothing ordinary about Gio, but I don't intend to say that.

'That's what I want. An ordinary guy. But one who is special to me. And who thinks I'm special too. Someone who'll love me, for me. Faults and all. Someone I can sit in silence with and not feel awkward, or chat for hours with and not be bored. Someone I can laugh with, cry with, share hopes and dreams with. Someone I can build a life with and who won't walk out on me, like Dad did, if things get tough, or if someone more attractive comes along. Someone who makes me tingle with the smallest touch, or look, or word. Someone whose kiss makes my toes curl with delight. Someone I long to make love with, day and night, anywhere anytime. Is that really too much to ask?'

He listens intently but raises his brows when I get to the tingle bit and they go higher and higher until there's nowhere else for them to go.

'Wow. That's some list. That's not an ordinary guy. That's a paragon.'

'No it's not. It's basically a friend who loves me and finds me so attractive that he wants to kiss me constantly. Well, maybe not constantly, but a lot. Know anyone like that?'

He stares into my eyes and I stare back.

'Let me think about it and I'll get back to you.'

'Fine. But don't wait too long. I've got five more dates tomorrow, as you rightly said. And according to the law of averages, they can't all be bad. In fact, they should all be good, because the five today, most assuredly were not.'

'So the wedding's off with Tim?'

I glare at him and he grins.

'At least you got some pretty flowers.'

I explain about the flowers and by .the time I finish, he's looking concerned and cross.

'I think Katie's right. You should ghost him. Or tell him you've changed your mind. Or you've met someone else. And you need to be careful, Emma. He's probably harmless and just a bit obsessive, but you never know. I want you to put my number in your phone and call me if you're scared, or you feel as if someone's following you, or you just need to talk. Okay?'

I nod. 'Okay.'

'And tomorrow, I want you to either come back here after every date, or at least text me to say you're fine.'

'Now I'm getting worried. Does everyone who dates online have to do all this?'

He shrugs. 'No idea. I've never tried it, but all we're doing is being sensible and making sure you're safe. It's no big deal. Until it is. So promise me, okay?'

'Okay. I promise.'

He tells me his number and I enter it into my phone and then I send him a text, saying, 'I'm okay. No need to worry. I'm with a guy I trust.'

He reads it when it pings through, and then he slowly lifts his head and smiles that gorgeous smile.

Nineteen

Thanks to Gio – and his Nonna's magic potion, my skin is almost as good as new when I wake up on Sunday morning. He gave me a tub of the miracle cream before I left La Dolce Vita yesterday evening, together with the other half of the cucumber, which he'd stored in his fridge.

'Smooth the paste over your face, close your eyes and cover them with cucumber slices, and then relax for at least five minutes,' he instructed.

'D'you want to come round and do it for me? I might not do it properly.'

I tried to persuade him with my best 'puppy-dog' eyes and he hesitated for a split second, but then he smirked.

'You're an intelligent woman. You'll be fine. Repeat it tomorrow morning and again on Sunday night.'

I followed his directions and I can't believe the difference. I could get away with not wearing any make-up today. But as I've got five dates, make-up is a must.

I soon discover the law of averages clearly does not apply to my dates.

The ones today are slightly better than yesterday, I suppose, but not enough to make much difference.

I start the day with Alan and I think things are looking up. The only troubling thing about him is that he's been married once already and then he was engaged. In both cases, no one else was involved with the break ups. He said he and his wife, and then he and his fiancée, just agreed they'd made a mistake.

He's either worryingly fickle, or he's exceptionally unlucky in love.

Other than that, he's nice, but I'm not sure he has potential. Although they do say, "third time lucky". Perhaps I could be his number three.

When we say goodbye, he doesn't mention seeing me again, so maybe not.

I send a text to Gio telling him I'm fine, that I'm waiting for my next date, and that I'll text him later.

Next is Owain. He's built like a rugby player, but as gentle as a kitten – and he actually has a kitten, he tells me.

'Cyril is a rescue and he thinks he rules the roost. He's only three months old but he's already seeing off my neighbour's dog, although when my neighbour pops in for a cuppa and brings Calypso, his Great Dane, with him, Cyril jumps up on his back and rides him as if the poor dog's a horse. And then they curl up together as if they're the best of friends. I love the little guy to bits.'

'He sounds wonderful,' I say, and Owain pulls out his phone and shows me some pictures of Cyril, and of Cyril riding Calypso and also some of the two of them curled up together.

Owain seems to be interested in me and he asks all the right questions. He's got a warm smile, a jolly laugh, and eyes that twinkle when he looks at me.

I like Owain.

He works for the local council in Brighton in the planning department and he loves his job.

He asks about mine and doesn't appear at all concerned that I have to travel a lot. When I say that I'm going to try to adopt a better work slash life balance, he merely smiles.

'I'm hoping to train up other members of my team,' I say. 'It's fantastic to get to go to so many different places, but living in hotels for weeks on end every few months does take a toll. And the reality is, I spend most of that time working, so I don't actually see much of wherever it is I am.'

'But it's an all-expenses paid taster, right? And you can then decide if that place is somewhere you'd want to return to or not.'

'Yes. Except the odd thing is, I can't remember the last time I took more than one day off from work. I have so many weeks holiday owed to me each year that the company has to insist I take at least some of it, so I do that at Christmas, or Easter, if I can. They allow me to carry over the rest, but I still don't take it, so ultimately, I end up losing it. But I don't mind.'

'I love my job but I take all my holiday time. And I get quite a lot. I love going away.'

We talk about our favourite places and our dream holiday destinations, and the one place we would go if money wasn't an issue.

'I'd go to another Universe,' he says. 'I'd love to know if there are other life forms out there somewhere.'

I don't bother to point out that, as far as his dream destination is concerned, money isn't the only thing stopping him.

'I'd go to a private island somewhere in the Caribbean.' It dawns on me as soon as I say it that that is precisely where my colleague, Ben is right now, so I add, 'or the South Pacific. Somewhere peaceful and remote, without my mobile phone or my laptop.'

He laughs at that. 'I don't think I could go anywhere without my mobile phone.'

I laugh too. 'You might not get a signal in another universe. I'm not sure any of the current networks cover outer space.'

I'm also not sure he finds that amusing, because there's a slight frown on his face now.

I wonder if I should apologise and tell him I'm only teasing, but if he can't handle that sort of banter, then Owain isn't the man for me, despite all his other good qualities.

'It's been fun,' he says, when I tell him I've got another date to meet fairly soon. 'If you'd like a second date, I'd be up for that.'

'I've had a good time. A second date might be nice. Shall we message one another via the dating site?'

He nods. 'Let's do that. We could go to see a film. Or to the theatre. We'll sort something out. Enjoy your next date.'

Owain smiles at me as he leaves, and I send a text to Gio.

'Date number seven is the best one yet.'

Gio sends me a thumbs up emoji in reply.

'Still not Mr Perfect,' I text back.

'Obviously not,' his reply states. 'Mr Perfect is right here.'

My heart thumps against my chest.

Is Gio saying he's *my* Mr Perfect? Or

simply that he *is* perfect?

And then I remind myself he's only teasing, either way.

Date number eight is Patrick, and he's absolutely gorgeous, just as he was in his photo. He struts towards me with a definite swagger and fixes me with an intense gaze. I feel a swoony sigh escaping, but he shatters the illusion when he speaks.

'All my friends call me Pat,' he says, 'so you can call me Patrick.'

He laughs like a drain, nudges me with his elbow, and asks where we can get a drink.

'Right there,' I say, feeling slightly bemused – and also a little bruised, as I point to La Dolce Vita.

'Crikey,' he says. 'I thought that only sold ice creams.'

'It's a bar, gelataria, coffee shop, and eatery. Basically, it covers all your needs.'

'I don't know about that,' he says, giving me a somewhat salacious, and also somewhat creepy, smile, along with another hard nudge. 'I have a lot of needs, if you get my drift?'

I definitely get his drift and I instantly decide he won't be getting any help with any of those from me.

In a tone my old and overly strict English teacher would have approved of, I say, 'Let's get that drink, shall we?'

He tells me he's an excellent judge of character, as we cover the short distance to La Dolce Vita, and that I've already ticked a few of the boxes on his list. I start to ask him which boxes they are, simply out of curiosity but he cuts me short.

'Do we have to queue to get a drink?' There are two long lines snaking from inside to outside.

'Sadly, yes. It's a popular place.'

'I hate queues. I hate waiting around for anything. Isn't there somewhere else we could go? Like your place perhaps?'

I raise my brows. 'I'm afraid not. We've only just met so that isn't an option. I don't intend to take anyone to my home until I feel I know them. That might take a few dates, or it might take several. I'm sure you understand.'

He shrugs. 'I suppose so. But it was worth a try.' And then he nudges me again and with an even more salacious smile, adds, 'You don't know what you're missing. I hope I'll get to see your place before too long.'

An abrupt, 'No', would be rude, so I prevaricate. 'I think that depends on how this date goes. I'm not making any promises. Shall we join one of the queues for that drink?'

He screws up his nose and glances at his smartwatch. 'Nah. They look like they go on forever and I've got to leave in half an hour. Rain check?'

I'm tempted to say, 'Fine. Call me when it rains', but I have no interest in seeing Patrick again, although I'm a little peeved he only set aside around thirty-five minutes for our date.

'Sure,' I say. 'If you're pushed for time, please don't let me keep you.'

'Really? Great. I'll be in touch then. This was great. You're great. And don't worry.' He winks and gives me yet another nudge. 'You've made it onto my list for a second date.'

'Oh, that is good news.'

I'm not sure if he detects the sarcasm in my voice, or not, but he raises both hands, closes them into fists, and gives me two thumbs up and a huge smile. I like to think I'm a reasonably fast learner, so I step back before he can give me a final nudge, and his elbow hits thin air.

'Bye, Patrick,' I say, stepping back a little farther.

He looks surprised before he hurries off.

I feel a bit deflated – in addition to slightly bruised, so I send Gio a text asking if he is free for lunch, and he immediately sends a reply telling me he is.

I'm more excited at the thought of spending time with him than I am with any of my dates. Maybe that should tell me something.

'One favourite and two more to go,' he says, once we're seated at a table with a 'reserved for staff' sign in the centre.

'Yep. But there are other sites to try, and I'm still waiting for one man from the current site to get back to me. He's the spitting image of a guy I work with, and I'm dying to know who he is.'

'You think it might be him? The guy you work with?'

I shake my head. 'I can't believe it is, especially as Ben is currently holidaying in the Caribbean with his gorgeous girlfriend. But this guy looks so much like Ben, that either he's a scammer, who has nicked Ben's photo from social media or somewhere, or he is Ben's doppelgänger.'

'Have you asked ... Ben about it?'

'No. I thought I'd wait and see if I receive another message from Leo. That's the guy's name on the dating website.'

'And if you do?'

I shrug. 'No idea. I haven't thought that far ahead, other than if it is a scammer, I'll either tell Ben about it, or I'll report Leo and his fake profile to the dating website. I've read that these websites take stuff like this very seriously now.'

'I believe they do. Well, a stalker and a

scammer? You certainly have good taste in men.'

I could take umbridge at his remark but I know he's teasing, and I laugh.

'Yeah. I've inherited that from Mum.'

I order a crunchy vegetable salad with shaved, raw asparagus and a Parmesan dressing and Gio orders the same.

We chat about everything and nothing over lunch and it's as if our disagreement of yesterday never happened. I'm a little disappointed when Gio says he should get back to work, and that it's probably time for my next date, but he's right.

Eddie is my next date.

He's tall, slim, and looks much younger in real life than in his profile photo. He's seriously into fishing, and although he's pleasant to talk to, somehow every topic of conversation manages to include something to do with fish.

I have never been fishing in my life and rightly or wrongly, it isn't something that's high on my list of things I must do before I'm forty.

So as nice as he is, I don't think I'll be seeing Eddie again.

My final date is Pete.

He's actually better looking than his profile photo. He is tall and well-built, and it's clear that he works out. He confirms this when he tells me he gets up at 6.00 a.m. every morning, including weekends, and alternates between a ten-mile run, a fifteen-mile cycle, or an hour at the gym. Sometimes he does all three in one day.

He looks genuinely horrified when I tell him that the only exercise I get is when I'm pottering in the garden, or I go for an occasional swim. But he's lovely, nonetheless.

Although when he informs me a little later that he never drinks alcohol, and doesn't date women who aren't prepared to limit their own intake to just one glass a day, I suggest that perhaps that is something he should make clear on his profile.

He doesn't take offence and we continue chatting for at least half an hour, even though, if we decide to take things further, our relationship will be doomed. I'm not addicted to alcohol, by any stretch of the imagination, but I am not prepared to limit myself to one glass of wine per day.

When he tells me that he assumes I already limit my consumption of chocolate and cake to fewer than one portion of each per week, I realise Pete is definitely not the man for me.

We both agree a second date probably isn't in either of our best interests.

'But if you're ever feeling lonely and

you're interested in a quick hook up, send me a message, and I'm your guy.'

I'm not offended by his comment, and I make a mental note that if I ever feel in need of a no strings attached night of passion, I could probably do worse than message Pete.

To be honest, when I say goodbye to him, I'm relieved I don't have to meet any further dates.

I make my way to La Dolce Vita and let myself in via the entrance at the rear. Gio has given me the code for the back door and it pops open the minute I tap in the numbers.

Gio is sitting at his desk, in that cosy little room and when I knock on the door and he looks up, he seems surprised to see me.

'Back so soon?'

'What can I say? No one took my breath away.'

He raises his brows. 'Did you think one of them might?'

I shrug. 'I'm an optimist. I had hope.'

'What's the plan from here?' He closes the accounts book he was writing in and leans back in his chair. 'Another dating site?'

I shrug again. 'I know that's what I said earlier, but to tell you the truth, this hasn't been as much fun as I thought it might. It wasn't something I had ever considered doing, or really thought through, until Katie and Nan suggested it, but I did think, once I had a list of all those dates, that meeting ten men would be both interesting and exciting. As it turns out, not so much.'

He grins. 'Lots of people have found love and happiness via the Internet, but personally, I think I'll stick to the old-fashioned way.'

'So you won't be joining any dating sites? Yesterday you said you thought you might.'

'I said a lot of things yesterday. Many of which I shouldn't have and some of which I regret.'

I'm about to ask him to be more specific when my phone rings, and glancing at the screen, I see it's Katie. I consider declining the call and phoning her later because I really want to continue this conversation with Gio, but I get the strangest feeling that I should take it. I don't even get a chance to say hello.

'Emma! You won't believe what's happened. Geneva's back. And she's threatening to sue Mack for breach of contract! He's taking it quite calmly, but Tori is beside herself.'

'What? Breach of contract! How can she do that?'

'I don't know. I'm not a lawyer. But I heard her say that he disclosed confidential information to competitors, enabling them to benefit from deals that were already in the advance stages of negotiation between

McBriar Properties and various parties.'

'Is she referring to Seascape Café?'

'I think so. Don't you? But Mack thinks it could also be in reference to Conqueror's Court, and Trulove Hotels.'

'What's Mack going to do?'

'He's going to discuss it with Portia Trulove, and see what she says.'

'I meant to tell you all yesterday that I saw Geneva. She was in La Dolce Vita, flirting with Gio.'

Gio is looking at me with concern in his eyes and confusion on his face.

'Yesterday?' Katie queries. 'I wonder why she waited until today to drop this bombshell?'

'Who knows? A woman like Geneva is capable of anything. Are you with Tori and Mack now?'

'Yes. And I'll be here for a while. I wanted to let you know about Geneva, but I also wanted to tell you that I won't be able to come round this evening to discuss your dates and decide on the next stage.'

'Don't worry about me. And I'm not even sure there will be a next stage. But we can discuss that another time. Give my love to Tori and Mack. And Katie, if there is anything I can do, give me a call.'

'What's happened?' Gio asks when I hang up, and he's astonished when I tell him.

'If I can be of any help, just let me know,' he says. 'Speaking of which...' He swivels in his chair, opens a mini fridge with a small freezer compartment inside, that is situated on a two-drawer filing cabinet behind him, swivels back to face me, and hands me a tub with La Dolce Vita's logo printed on the side.

'More miracle cream?' I ask.

'Yes,' he says, grinning. 'But don't put these on your face.'

I lift the lid a fraction to see what's inside.

'Ooh, Bacio and Pistacchio! I exclaim with delight as I see a large scoop of each. 'They're my favourites.'

'I know,' he says, and there's something in his eyes that makes my insides turn to slush.

Twenty

I receive various messages on Monday from some of my dates over the weekend, via the dating website, but due to Ben being on holiday, meaning I'm doing more work than usual, and the situation with Mack and Tori, I'm not really in the mood to arrange second dates. Not that there are many I'm considering for second dates.

After checking the messages late on Monday evening, there are five from Tim, so he is definitely off the list. I send him a brief message, thanking him for the flowers, but saying he really shouldn't have done that, and that due to a change of circumstances, I won't be able to consider seeing him again. I wish him well and thank him once more for the flowers. I hope that will be the last contact Tim and I will have.

I really can't be bothered reading the rest right now so I decide to send messages to all the men I met, saying that due to work commitments I won't be able to answer messages until Saturday, and I post a note on my profile saying I'm temporarily unavailable for dates. That way there will be no confusion. I'll sort it out at the weekend. But just as I'm about to sign out, a message arrives from Leo – the one who looks like Ben. And that one I do have to read.

'Sorry I haven't been in touch,' it says, 'but my gran fell ill and I had to rush to see her. Sadly she passed away and I'm completely devastated. I don't know what day of the week it is, or what I'm doing, and to make things worse, my bank account has been frozen due to some sort of suspicious activity on my card. Don't you hate these scammers? Anyway, I need to try to sort something out to get some cash, so as much as I really want to see you, unless I can get my finances sorted, I won't be able to right now. Such a pity because I think you and I are the perfect fit, don't you? My gran would've loved you. I'm so sad that she won't get to meet you. I wish I had your phone number so that we could chat. I'm feeling so lost and lonely and I know your lovely voice would cheer me up. I can tell your voice will be lovely and that you're a kind and caring person from your profile.'

I have to stop reading at that point although it goes on and on. Leo is clearly a scammer and he's hoping to get my number, and to make me feel 'special' and convince me we've made a real connection, so that he can persuade me to send him some money. I'm going to report him to the website and as soon as Ben gets back, I'll tell him all about Leo and his profile photo.

But I just can't help myself. I must send Leo a message.

'So sorry about your gran, Leo,' I say, 'and your bank account too. How dreadful. And yes. I do hate scammers!'

Bloody online dating. The last thing I want to think about right now is men!

That's not entirely true. There is one man I can't stop thinking about.

Possibly two.

Gio.

And Ben.

Ben has a girlfriend, so he won't be dating me. Gio doesn't, but he's made it pretty clear, he won't be dating me either.

And then I see more messages are waiting for me on the dating site, and although I want to turn off my laptop and go to bed, I scroll through to see them. Fifteen new messages are in my inbox. And every one of them is from Tim. He must be an incredibly fast typist. And he must have a lot to say.

I read the first and then the second and

then skip to the last. Each one is increasingly angry. Each one accuses me of not telling the truth. Each one says I led him on. I definitely did no such thing. What is wrong with the man?

I am about to delete them all when I decide that, in addition to Leo, perhaps I should report Tim. Everyone was right about him. Red flags are flapping like crazy.

I feel mean, somehow, but men should not treat women as if they are possessions, or get cross when things don't go as men had hoped or planned. I send off the reports, and then immediately turn off my laptop. I realise I still haven't read the other messages and they too might say horrid things, so I wonder now if I should read them, but I'm tired and annoyed and I decide I couldn't care less right now. I'm not going to look at that site again until the weekend.

The rest of the week is so hectic that I really don't have time to think about anything other than work in any case, not even Tori and Mack, although I do text Katie once or twice asking how things are going. We're getting together at Seascape Café tonight and I'm meeting Katie and Aaron there, because I'm running late at work.

When I arrive, Katie, Aaron, Tori and Mack are all huddled around a table in the sitting room of Tori's flat above the café. Lou and Dave have come in to help in the café this evening, so that Tori and Mack can have a much-needed evening off.

'Portia has been an absolute star,' Tori says, as I catch up on what I've missed.

Mack nods in agreement. 'Portia's told me not to worry. She's instructed not just her lawyers, but also an independent lawyer to act for me. And she's going to foot the bill. I don't think Geneva or her dad expected Portia to support me and to have my back. My lawyer has told me that he's convinced McBriar Properties will drop their claim. The sooner they do that, the less it'll cost them in the long run, and money is their God, so we're all hoping that by next week, we'll have some good news.'

'That's wonderful,' I say.

Tori and Mack smile at one another and hold each other's hands.

'We're not out of the woods yet,' says Mack. 'But at least we're on the right path. And you'll never believe this, but after all these years, my grandfather has been in contact. That's been an even bigger surprise than Geneva's lawsuit. He's sent two letters via his solicitors. One to Vida and one to me. They know where Vida lives because they handled the purchase of Vida's cottage when I came into my inheritance. Both letters are similar, as if he couldn't be bothered thinking of anything much to say to either of us and was simply going through the motions. Basically, he says that he thinks it's time we all considered putting the past behind us. He's unwell, so both letters say, and he wants to 'put things right before going to his grave'. I was tempted to tell him it's too late, but then I thought about my dad and I wondered what he and Mum would want. Both Vida and I are still undecided to be honest, and there's no love lost between my grandfather and me, but I suppose there's no harm in seeing him.' He shrugs.

'Wow! That really is a surprise,' I say. I think, after what Mack told us about his grandfather and the awful way the man behaved, it might be difficult for Mack and Vida to forgive him, and if they both told him to get lost, no one would blame either of them.

'What about you, Emma?' Tori asks. 'Any news on the dating front?'

'Other than me thinking that one of the men I met over the weekend may have some serious issues, not really.' I tell them about the messages from Tim and that Leo clearly was a fake account. 'I'm going to tell Ben when he's back in the office on Monday. He should know someone is using a photo of him to try to defraud women out of money.'

'So are you arranging to meet more

men?' Mack asks. Or do you no longer see online dating as the solution to your love life?'

'I'm not sure I ever did. It was Katie and Nan who suggested it.'

'We were trying to help,' Katie says defensively. 'And they can't all be bad. There must be some nice guys on these sites.'

'I know you were,' I say. 'And I appreciate your help. And Nan's. But I'm not sure online dating is for me. I was exhausted after the weekend and so glad to get back to work on Monday. I haven't really had time to think about it this week. I'm going to take a look tomorrow and I'll decide from there.'

'Perhaps you should look closer to home,' Tori says. 'Like inside La Dolce Vita.'

'What?'

She grins at me. 'Word travels fast in Norman Landing, you should know that.'

Katie looks confused. 'Are you suggesting Emma should date Giovanni Russo? Or are you simply saying there are lots of single men who go there and could be potential dates?'

Tori tuts and rolls her eyes. 'Giovanni, obviously.'

'Why obviously?' Katie asks, but she's not as shocked as I thought she would be by that idea.

'Because they clearly like one another.'

'Do they?' Katie looks at me. 'Do you like him, Emma?'

I'm suddenly feeling flustered. 'I like him, yes.'

'Do you want to date him?' Mack queries.

'We don't always get what we want.'

'So it *is* true!' says Katie. 'Nan said she thought you might be interested in 'the Russo boy' and I told her she was imagining it. I'm not sure she'll be thrilled.'

'She needn't worry. He's made it clear he won't be dating me.'

'What's he said?' Tori asks.

'Nothing really. That's the problem. Just that, due to the past, it wouldn't work between us.'

'What happened back then?' Tori looks from me to Katie. 'We'd moved to Brighton long before he left so, although you and I were still best friends, I missed out on all the drama. I knew something had gone on because one minute we all hung out together and the next, no one would talk about Giovanni Russo. It was as if merely saying his name would conjure up the devil or make something really bad happen. Like in those horror films, when if you say a name or a word, and someone dies a horrific death.'

Katie shakes her head. 'I don't really know either. As you say, we all used to hang

189

out together. Then one day, Mum told Emma and me we were never to see him again. A few weeks later, he was gone. And you're right, Tori. No one would mention him or talk about him at all. His mum died when he was young. That's why he lived with his gran. And I know from Nan that his dad was in prison, and we all knew that Giovanni was always getting into trouble. Nothing serious. Just little things. And then he stole something big, so Nan says, and he lied about it. Charges were never brought and it was all hushed up, but I think it had something to do with Holy Trinity Church.'

I'm cringing as I'm listening to them. I want to shout it out right here and now. I want to tell them all the truth. But I promised Gio I would speak to him about it again before I did anything, so I bite my tongue and hope no one says something to make me react in a way I may regret.

'I heard Giovanni owns La Dolce Vita,' says Tori. 'I assumed he was working there, for Alberto and Silvio, but no. He owns it.'

'Who told you that?' asks Katie.

'I heard Alberto talking to Dave the other day. Lou and Dave are off on holiday soon and they're going somewhere in Italy where Alberto still has relatives, so Dave's taking some gifts over for Alberto. Anyway, he popped in to drop them off, and he told Dave that he was pleased Giovanni had decided to buy La Dolce Vita and to return to Norman Landing. He said it's what Giovanni's Nonna would've wanted.'

'Where did Giovanni get the money from?' Katie queries. 'The Russos weren't rich. In fact, they were as poor as we were, after our dad left.'

'Probably stole it.' Tori bursts out laughing.

'He didn't steal it!' I can't take any more of this. 'He went to the States, started his own business, worked really hard, and sold it so that he could buy La Dolce Vita and come back here to make a fresh start.'

'Oooh! Keep your shirt on.' Tori grins at me and then she narrows her eyes. 'How do you know all that, Emma Barr?'

I cast my gaze down to the table top, and twist my wine glass around with my fingers. 'Gio told me.'

'And you believe him?' Mack's tone suggests he's simply seeking clarification, not that he doubts my words.

'Absolutely.' I raise my eyes to his. 'I trust him with my life.'

'Wow!' Katie stares at me. 'That's a bit dramatic, Emma.'

Aaron, who hasn't said very much at all this evening, suddenly pipes up. 'I think Emma knows a lot about Giovanni Russo.

Far more than you would possibly have imagined, I suspect.'

Everyone looks at me expectantly.

'I do. You're right. And he knows a lot about me. Things you wouldn't believe. I want to tell you everything. But I made him a promise and until I talk to him about it, it's a promise I can't break. I let him down very badly fifteen years ago. I can't do that to him again.'

'You said you never slept with him!' Tori points her finger at me.

'I never did. That's the truth. Not everything that happens between a man and a woman, or in this case, two teenagers as we were then, is about sleeping together. Sometimes it's about far more important things. Like loyalty, honour, courage, betrayal, sacrifice, trust. About believing in someone when everyone else has cast them out. About forgiveness. And about love. Real love.'

'Okay.' Tori refills my glass of wine. 'Now you've got to tell us what you know.'

I shake my head. 'No I don't. Because I know how to keep a secret.'

Twenty-one

Luckily for me, I rarely have to work weekends, unless I'm at a new clients' supervising a new installation, but I get a call at an ungodly hour on Saturday morning asking if I can fly up to Edinburgh and placate a prospective client with whom Ben had been dealing. The client hasn't signed up yet and wasn't happy to discover that Ben was away last week, and has now decided that, unless someone from our company visits them today to answer some last-minute questions, they'll go elsewhere.

Julian, the guy who called me from Ben's team, is having a bit of a breakdown over the phone and is apologising profusely for phoning me at 7 a.m. I can hear Ben's voice saying, 'DEFCON2, Em,' but I know he would be smiling. We've both heard threats like this before and the prospective clients rarely mean it.

'Don't panic, Julian,' I say. 'And don't

apologise for calling. While Ben's still away, that's what I'm here for. But Ben and I have dealt with this sort of thing before and it's probably not as serious as you think. Firstly, this client is behaving like a petulant child and is probably hoping they'll get some kind of discount, that's all. I can handle that. Secondly, our software is the best of its kind, and the client will know that, so it's unlikely they'll walk away. Unless the issue is they've realised they can't afford our product, in which case, it's best if they do walk away.'

'Thanks, Emma. So what should I do? Freddie's sick with that stomach bug he had yesterday. I called him first before I disturbed you. I also tried Lydia, but she's not answering.'

I don't blame her. Freddie, the one who is unwell, is Ben's number two, and his number three, Lydia, is about to give birth any day, so although I would've sent one of those two, a guy vomiting over the desk during a negotiation, or a woman's water breaking on the floor of the client's conference room, probably won't help. There's really only one option. I'm not sure who else Ben would send in a case like this.

'Email me all the details, please, Julian, and get me on a flight this morning. Oh, and have a car pick me up and take me to the airport. I was drinking last night so I can't drive.' Thankfully, my company wouldn't expect me to take public transport. 'Then leave it with me. I'll get it sorted, one way or the other.'

'Really? Oh wow! Thank you, Emma! You're a life saver.'

'It's my job, Julian, so no thanks necessary. Book me that flight and then go and make yourself a coffee and have a biscuit and a break, okay?'

'Roger that,' he says, reminding me of Ben yet again.

I groan and turn over in bed. I was looking forward to this weekend. I was going to check into that dating site again and decide if I want to arrange any second dates, assuming any of the men I liked also want that. Although as there was really only Owain, now that Tim is a no-no, and possibly one other, that won't take long anyway.

I was also going to see if the company had sent me a message regarding the two accounts I'd reported. I could still do that too, either in the car on the way, or at the airport.

I'll have to read the client's file on the flight, so that all the details are fresh in my head when I arrive in Edinburgh. I try to think who the client could be but we have several in negotiations and until they sign on the dotted line, Ben's team handles them.

While Ben's away, I'm only involved if there's an issue – as there is right now.

A few minutes later, I get a text from Julian with details of the car and my flight, saying 'email with files to follow' and thanking me again.

I drag myself out of bed and get into the shower, after which, I pull my damp hair into a chignon and apply a smattering of make-up. I always have a natural look for work, which is often harder to achieve, but as I've got a bit of a tan, thanks to last weekend on the pier, it doesn't take long today. That's just as well, as I've only got time for a quick coffee, and to text Katie and Nan to tell them where I'll be, before the car arrives. I've thrown a few things into a carry-on, overnight bag, just in case, so I can have breakfast at the airport as I don't have to faff around with luggage. When I'm on a trip for work, a company collects my luggage and sends it on ahead, and then returns it home for me, unless I change my plans and return a few days early, as I have done recently. But on the rare occasions last minute travel is necessary, like today, I deal with my own luggage.

I check the dating site once I'm settled in the back seat of the car and there is a message from the company about my reports. It simply says they're looking into the matters and will respond in more detail shortly. A pretty standard reply, I assume.

And then I see I have a couple of other messages in addition to those I left unanswered, including one from Tim. I decide to leave his until last, after those horrid ones on Monday, and as my phone beeps with a text right at that second, I look at that instead.

It's ridiculous, I know, but my heart leaps in my chest when I see it is from Gio.

'Hi Emma, Hope you've had a good week. I expect you'll have a list of men lined up for this weekend, but fancy a coffee? I can recommend a place at the end of the pier, if you can squeeze me into your hectic schedule.'

I'm smiling from ear to ear but I simply can't help it. This had made me ridiculously happy.

'Sorry. I can't. On my way to Scotland.'

I haven't finished, but the car hits a pothole in the road and my finger slips to send. Damn it! I'm typing the rest but this road is like a minefield and my predictive text is inserting words that don't make sense so I'm having to keep deleting them. I'm still typing when another text arrives.

'Gretna Green? May I be the first to wish you every happiness? Bit sudden though. Sure this is The One? Or have you been abducted? Willing to ride to your rescue if you need me. Any idea where I'd find a white horse?'

My heart sings with joy and this time I'm careful as I type.

'Sorry. Hit send in error. Was going to say I've got to work. Haven't been abducted. Not eloping. Wouldn't mind being rescued. Try CCS. I'm sure Mr Williams will sell horses. Can come for coffee when I get back. Not sure when though.'

I eagerly await a reply and I'm like a kid at Christmas. I don't have long to wait.

'Relieved on all counts. Will order horse today. Just in case. Welcome for coffee whenever. Text me. Enjoy bonnie Scotland. But not too much. And avoid any handsome men in kilts.'

Without thinking, I text back: 'Will avoid all men in kilts if you'll avoid all women in bikinis, or beautiful women wanting ice cream.'

I wait. And I wait. And I wait. But there's no reply to that.

Have I gone too far? Does he think I'm telling him to stay away from other women? But he told me to avoid handsome men in kilts.

Should I text again saying I was joking? But then he'll know I'm worried.

It's only then I see there is no signal on

my phone, but a few minutes later another text from him arrives.

'Deal. Will avoid all women except for one. Mr Williams is completely out of horses. Will try Tesco. Hope to see you soon.'

The driver almost swerves as I shriek with delight.

'I'm so, so sorry,' I say, 'but I think I've just had some very good news.'

'That's lovely. I nearly had a heart attack, but we're all good.'

I apologise again and then send Gio a final text.

'Definitely see you soon. Have a good weekend.'

I lean back and close my eyes, completely forgetting about the dating website and what I was doing when I got Gio's first text and instead I imagine all sorts of scenarios involving me and Gio. We're in the cold-room, and in his cosy office, and on his desk, and even on the back of a stunningly gorgeous white horse.

I'm not sure if Gio is just teasing, or if he really is interested in me, but I realise I am interested in him. I knew I was, of course, but until this morning, I hadn't really realised quite how much. I care about him now even more than I did all those years ago – and I cared about him a lot in those days.

I hung on his every word, his every look.

I wanted him to like me, really like me. To see me as a young, attractive, desirable woman and not the fifteen-year-old girl I was. I wanted to show him I didn't care about his dad being in prison, I didn't care what people thought of him. I wanted to do the things he did. To show him I didn't care what people thought of me either. I wanted to impress him. Which is partly why I made such a mess of things that day.

I wanted him to be in my life for ever. Instead, my actions resulted in him being sent away. To America, as I recently discovered.

But now he's back. And now I am a woman. Whether he finds me attractive and desirable only he can say, but the way he looks at me sometimes makes me think he does. And the things he says, make me think so too. Those texts today, definitely make me think so.

There is no doubt that I find him exceedingly attractive and utterly desirable. So what is the point in pretending I don't?

And even if he is just teasing (which I truly hope is not the case) and all we'll ever be is just friends, I know something for certain. None of those men I met last weekend, could ever make me feel the way Gio does.

Ben can. But he's got a girlfriend.

These other men? No way. I may have only met them once, and very briefly, but there wasn't a spark. I liked Owain the most, but I couldn't really care if I ever see him again or not.

So I make a decision. I'm going to tell those men I met over the weekend, with the exception of Tim, that I've realised I may have feelings for someone I knew in the past, who has recently come back into my life. I'm going to say how good it was to meet them and how lovely they all are. Even though some of them aren't, in my opinion at least. And I'm going to say I'm no longer available for dates. I'll wish them all well and then I'll delete my account. And I'll do that as soon as I arrive at the airport. Or maybe after my breakfast, as my stomach is rumbling now, and my laptop needs to go on charge.

I've already checked in for my flight via my phone, so I go in search of food after I get out of the car and thank the driver for our safe journey. As a frequent flyer, I have access to any of the lounges, although passes can be purchased for most of them these days, but I really want a full English breakfast to set me up for the day. I'm not sure what today has in store and when I'll get a chance to eat, so by filling up now, I can work through no matter what. I go to my favourite restaurant and order the works, including toast and marmalade.

I take a seat at a table and plug in my laptop. The first thing I do is go back to the dating site. I've already read the message from the company so I ignore that. Apart from the message from Tim, there're a couple of others, two of which are from Owain, so I read those first.

The one sent on Sunday, shortly after our date on Sunday morning, simply says he had fun and would like to see me again, so if I still feel the same, we can think about where we'd like to meet and catch up later in the week.

The second, sent on Thursday, thanks me for the update I sent on Monday. It confirms he liked me and that he had a good time, but I smile as I read on, because it seems Owain has met someone. Not via the website, he says, but at his local Indian restaurant.

He went there with his mates on Sunday night, the day we met, and Lucy, a girl he was at school with years ago, was at the restaurant with some friends. It seems both sets of friends merged tables, and by the end of the evening, Owain and Lucy had arranged to meet up the very next day. He's seen her every day since then and he is deleting his account from the dating site.

'Yay!' I say aloud, forgetting where I am.

I send him a message back wishing him and Lucy all the very best and telling him I'm in a similar situation although mine has not yet had the same wonderful conclusion but I'm hoping for the best. I'm genuinely pleased for him. And for Lucy, even though I have never met her.

The next message is from Pete, the fitness fanatic, reminding me if I ever fancy a hook up, he's my man. I consider sending him a thumbs up emoji, but I remember I'm deleting my account, so instead I send him the message I'm intending to send to everyone, other than Tim, of course.

There's a message from Alan, the one who is either fickle or very unlucky in love. He says he's happy to see me again but he's not convinced it'll lead to anything. I send him the same message I sent Pete.

To my astonishment, there's one from Paul, the man with the gold teeth. His mum's invited me round for tea, and to show me some of her tatts. I shiver at the thought of meeting his mum, and immediately send the now 'standard' message.

There's one from Eddie, asking me if I'd like to go fishing. I send him my standard message.

And there's one from Patrick, the serial nudger, saying he thinks we might've got off on the wrong foot but he's willing to give me a second chance. I send the standard message. And then there's the one from Tim. I take a deep breath before reading it, but it still makes me gasp. It simply says, 'You'll be sorry.'

I'm so stunned, because it sounds a bit like a threat, and in my surprise, I forget, and I send him the standard message.

I am relieved when I press the button to delete my account.

Online dating works for many, but I am definitely not one of them.

Twenty-two

What is going on today? I feel as if I'm on a roller coaster. One minute down, the next up, then a slight flattening out followed by down again. Only now it seems it's continuing a downward trajectory. The phone call from Julian, was the first downer. The texts from Gio were a soaring high. Then came the messages from Owain, the main one of which was lovely and another high, and then the messages from the others, which didn't really have an impact. And then came the message from Tim, and it's only getting worse from there.

Tim's message had unnerved me, but not as much as when I took my seat on the plane and opened the email from Julian with details of the client I'm going to see.

Surely this can't be true?

I've got to be at the offices of McBriar Properties for a meeting with Mr McBriar and Geneva McBriar at 12 noon on the dot.

Quite what makes me think of an old western, Mum, Katie, Nan, and I used to watch on rainy Sunday afternoons, I'm not sure, but it could be because the film was called High Noon. If I remember correctly, it's about a gun fight between the local Marshall and the baddies, and the people of the town being too cowardly to help. I'm hoping I'm the 'good guy' in this scenario. But I'm definitely going to face the McBriars alone, and no one is coming to my aid.

The problem is, although Geneva doesn't know who I am, there is potentially a conflict of interest, because I'm the sister of Tori's best friend, and Tori is dating Mack, who McBriar Properties are suing. This could easily end up as the equivalent of a nuclear explosion. I really should call my boss and tell him, in case it does all blow up. I can hear Ben saying, 'We're at DEFCON2, Em, and the slightest wrong move could mean DEFCON1. Might be wise to retreat and regroup.'

Ben will be back on Monday. I'm tempted to get off the plane and say I've come down with something. Maybe the tummy bug that Freddie has. But before I have a chance to decide, the engines roar, the jetway retracts, and the plane begins to taxi from the gate.

Now there is nothing I can do, other than phone my boss later and explain the situation, or meet the McBriars today, hope Geneva won't recognise me, and hand it over to Ben first thing on Monday morning.

I read the file and decide I must be right; the McBriars are surely after a discount. I can't see anything in the file that could have caused an issue. As far as I can see, until that email Julian called me about, negotiations were progressing as normal. Why is it that the wealthiest clients in the world are usually the ones who want the discounts, whereas the poorer clients pay what is asked without quibbling? Nan would probably say that is how the richest companies became so rich. I find it rather annoying.

The more I read about McBriar Properties and the conversations the McBriars have had with Ben, the less I like them. It's clear they want everything their own way and expect us to jump through hoops backwards. We always go out of our way to provide any tweaks the clients may want, within reason, but I get the impression Geneva is simply seeing how far she can push. I think Ben thought the same, judging by his last email and the notes he made. I'm the one who'll have to be there to supervise the installation, if they go ahead. Do I really want to spend time in the company of Geneva and possibly her dad? That is a definite no.

I have the authority to negotiate discounts up to a certain amount. Perhaps I should tell the McBriars there will not be a discount. That might make them go elsewhere.

But as I told Julian this morning, we have the best software in our business, so I'm not sure it'll be that simple. And the McBriars can, of course, go over my head and directly to my boss. What will he say if he discovers I haven't given them the discount he is always happy to allow?

I phone my boss once I'm in the car on the way to the meeting in Edinburgh. I apologise for calling him and explain the situation. To my astonishment, he's not that bothered.

'Technically, yes, there's a conflict of interest,' he says, 'but that only matters if we don't tell them, and then they can prove we have given them a bad deal, or treated them in a way we wouldn't treat our other clients. That won't happen so I don't see it as a problem. And you can handle it, Emma. I have the utmost confidence in you. I think it's wise to come clean right at the outset, just to be on the safe side. If they don't want to continue negotiations, that's up to them. But you and I both know we're the best there is, so I think they'll soon come back to us. It can't be due to lack of money. McBriar

Properties is one of the richest companies in the UK. But call me if you need me. I don't want you to feel you're in an uncomfortable situation. Especially not after Toronto.'

I thank him, and feel better than I did. He supported me without question when that creep in Toronto propositioned me and tried to grope me in a lift. I know he'll do the same now. That's one of the reasons I love working for this company. They really do put their employees first.

By the time I reach the towering building that's home to McBriar Properties, I'm ready for Geneva and her dad and whatever they might throw at me.

But I've underestimated Geneva. She recognises me the moment I walk in and although she doesn't say so, I can see it in her eyes. And when she asks her dad if they might have a word, and asks me to excuse them for a moment, I know that something is up.

I'm even more certain, when she returns ten minutes later without him, looking cool, calm and collected, and very much in charge. She's dressed casually, but expensively from head to toe and it irks me a little that her earrings alone could probably buy one hundred suits like the one I'm wearing. And I don't buy cheap clothes. I earn an exceptionally good salary and receive benefits on top, but Geneva no doubt spends my annual salary on one single shopping spree. I'm not jealous, but I do feel a little ill at ease, and that is most unlike me.

She tells me she's arranged for us to have lunch, because, she says, she wasn't sure if I have eaten.

'That's very kind,' I say, 'but I had a large breakfast, and I couldn't eat a thing, although I wouldn't say no to some coffee.'

'As you wish,' she says.

She doesn't take her eyes off me while a young and rather good-looking man pours both of us a cup, in what is clearly exceedingly expensive bone china with a wide, gold band around the middle. I'm immediately reminded of Paul and his gold teeth, and I almost burst out laughing. Thankfully I manage to control myself.

She waits until the young man has gone and then she crosses her exceptionally long legs, rests one forearm on the arm of her chair, and the other on the massive conference table and smiles the coldest smile I think I've ever seen.

'We meet again, Emma Barr,' she says.

I hold her stare and jut out my chin. 'Indeed we do, Geneva McBriar.'

She obviously knows my name because Julian would have told the McBriars I would be representing the company today, but whether or not she put my name together with Tori's best friend's sister, or even the woman she saw in La Dolce Vita that day, or whether those connections have just dawned on her, I do not know. Yet somehow I suspect she knows a lot more than I can guess.

One perfectly shaped eyebrow quirks up a fraction but is quickly pulled under control.

'Is this at all awkward?' she asks, still staring.

'Not in the least,' I say, hoping I am not the first to blink. 'I have discussed this with my boss and we do not believe there is a conflict of interest but I want to be clear from the off. My sister is the best friend of Mackenzie Fisher's girlfriend, Tori, and I am aware of the claim your company has issued against him.'

Now both brows shoot up. 'I wasn't aware of that,' she says.

But I can tell she was. I think Geneva McBriar has done her research, or more likely, paid others to do it, and knows everything there is to know about her ex-fiancé's (fake or not) new girlfriend, Tori, and therefore, my sister, and no doubt, myself. And possibly anyone else who knows Mack. Partly because, that's probably what I would have done if I had her money.

'Really?' I say. 'I'm surprised by that. I would've thought any savvy business woman would have done her research.' I know I shouldn't have said that but I really don't like Geneva and her 'I'm so much better than you' attitude.

Her eyes narrow and she shifts a fraction in her chair and then the icy smile reappears. I get the distinct feeling that I'm a doomed ship that's about to hit an iceberg.

'You aren't easily intimidated, are you, Emma?'

'No, Geneva. I'm not.'

'You're right about me being a savvy business woman,' she says. 'I get that from my dad. I've also got his ruthlessness where business is concerned.'

I wait for her to continue but she doesn't so I say, 'Just where business is concerned?'

She fixes me with her steely gaze. 'No. You said you wanted to be clear from the off, and I appreciate that. So let me do the same. I know everything there is to know about Mack's new girlfriend. And about everyone else who knows him, or her. And I do mean everything, Emma. I know this because I like to get my own way. And if someone ... displeases me, as Mack has, I make it my business to ensure I return that displeasure, tenfold. And that's what I intend to do. Why do you think I sent that email while your colleague, Ben is away?'

That is a surprise. I quickly run the

scenario through in my head.

'So this meeting has nothing to do with the software. It's all about Mack and ... revenge? I saw your company contacted us about purchasing our product the month before Mack came to Norman Landing. The head of your IT department was handling negotiations. It's only fairly recently that you have personally become involved. But I don't see what you hope to gain from this. The company I work for has no connection with Mack. And I have no influence over him. So why have you brought me here?'

'It's very simple, Emma. I want ... this company wants ... to acquire several properties in Norman Landing. Mack's recent foolishness has ... put a small spanner in the works. But I still want those properties. Perhaps more so now. I want Conqueror's Court, Seacroft Cottage, and everything along the shore, from Barnard's Christmas Tree Farm, to Seascape Café and beyond, because there's also another property I now want. La Dolce Vita. Possibly, the entire pier. I haven't decided yet.'

I bristle at that. Who does this woman think she is?

'Sadly, Geneva, this is not a game of Monopoly. You can't simply decide you want to buy these properties and then expect to get them. Seascape Café is under new ownership, Trulove Hotels has as good as signed on the dotted line for the purchase of Conqueror's Court, Seacroft Cottage is not for sale and neither is La Dolce Vita. Nor is the pier, as far as I'm aware. Barnard's Christmas Tree Farm, may or may not be. But I still don't see what any of this has to do with me. Or why I'm here.'

'Because I think you may be able to ... persuade some of the players that they should sell to me. And yes it is a game, Emma. Not of Monopoly, but a game all the same. And when I play games, I like to win.'

I snort derisively. I can't help it. I think this woman watches too many TV dramas. Does she honestly believe she can manipulate people into doing what she wants?

'As fascinating as this is,' I say. 'Unless you want to discuss the software I'm here about, there really is no point in me staying.'

'You love your job, don't you?'

That takes me by surprise. 'Yes. I do.'

'How would you feel if you lost it?'

'Lost my job?' I have no idea where she is going with this. 'I don't know. But as that isn't likely to happen, it's not something to which I've given any thought.'

'I have. And this is how I see things playing out. I want Mack to walk away from Trulove Hotels and the Conqueror's Court deal and to come back to work for me. We can beat the Trulove bid, together. I also want him to sell me Seacroft Cottage. I want Tori and the Simpkins to sell me Seascape Café, and I want Giovanni to sell me La Dolce Vita.'

'None of which, I'm sorry to have to inform you, is ever going to happen.'

'I can make all your lives very difficult. Tori and Mack's, your sister's, yours, and, of course, the very handsome, Gio's.'

I'm getting cross. Geneva McBriar has a screw lose. That's the only explanation. But she has dragged me here under false pretences and has ruined my weekend. I could be having coffee now, with Gio.

I get to my feet with a sigh. 'Well, Geneva, this has been ... fun. But there is somewhere else I'd rather be, so I'll say good luck with all of that, and I'll wish you a good day.'

I turn to walk away but her next words stop me dead.

'I think Tori would do anything to help her friends. And Mack, as foolish as he is, seems to genuinely believe he's in love with her, so he will do anything for Tori. I need him to see how ridiculous that is and to come back to me immediately. Katie would hate to see you unhappy, and Tori is Katie's best friend. You are in love with Giovanni and he is clearly in love with you, so you will do anything for one another. Do you see where I'm going with this now, Emma? You all have secrets. Things from your pasts you'd all rather other people didn't know. But let's focus on you for now. How sad would it be if your boss, and all your company's clients, discovered you are in love with a criminal? And what would happen to La Dolce Vita and Gio, if everyone in Norman Landing and way beyond, found out what Gio did all those years ago? It was all hushed up back then but I'm not sure it could be hushed up now. I know everything there is to know about all of you. Because you're right, Emma. I do my research. Or more accurately, I pay the very best people in the business to do that research for me. And I know exactly how to cause you all the most pain possible, until I get what I want. And what I want is Mack. And all those properties in Norman Landing.'

She really is insane. Or maybe, I suddenly realise, she is an incredibly sad and lonely woman who has lost the man she loves to someone else and is so eaten up with jealousy and rage that she's lashing out at everyone and everything she can. But what she has said about Gio, unnerves me the most. And yet it also gives me strength.

'Yes, Geneva, we do all have secrets. I'm

sure you have some of your own. Some that you would rather other people didn't find out. And while I'm not rich enough to employ the people you do, I do have friends of friends who are. I'm sure they would be happy to help once they hear what you've threatened. As for my boss and our clients, I think they'll give me the benefit of the doubt, because they trust me. And I have other news for you. You're not quite as well informed as you think you are concerning Gio. Plus, you underestimate Portia Trulove if you think she'll simply walk away. She's a lovely, loyal person, and Mack will not let her down, just as she won't let him down, so you can forget about him coming back to you. That isn't going to happen. And yes, he does love Tori, and I'll tell you why. She is also lovely and she cares about other people. Something you might want to try. It might make you feel better and happier than seeking revenge ever will. I think this is all about the fact that Mack didn't love you, and that he left you without a second thought. Let me give you some free advice. Stop trying to hurt people to get what you want and try being nice to them for a change. You'll find you attract more bees with honey than with vinegar. As for the properties in Norman Landing, you will never get them. If Barnards Christmas Tree Farm is still up for sale, the

217

aforementioned friends of my friends will happily purchase it to ensure you can't. I have no doubt of that either. And if you defame Gio by spreading gossip and untruths, everyone in Norman Landing will support him. We'll all make certain of that.'

She glowers at me for a second or two and I can see from the expression on her face that she is angry and that she hadn't expected my reaction. She probably expected me to cower at her feet.

'You seem very sure of yourself,' she says, having managed to regain her composure.

'I am, Geneva. And I'll tell you why. I have friends and family who love me and will support me no matter what, as I will them. And my friends have people who love them and will support them no matter what. So you see, it isn't just me, and Katie, and Tori, and Mack, and Gio, you will be taking on. You'll be taking on Portia Trulove, and an entire army of friends of us all. And added to that, you'll be taking on the whole of Norman Landing. I'm not sure you want to do that. One of the most important things about business, and about love, is knowing when to cut your losses and move on. Perhaps, instead of wasting your time and energy, along with everyone else's, just to seek revenge, you might be better off taking a good hard look at yourself and your life. Do you have friends and family who love you? Really love you. Who will do anything for you, no matter what. I somehow doubt it. Believe me, Geneva, all the money in the world won't buy you that. I mean this in a good way, be nicer, Geneva. Be better than this. You're an incredibly beautiful woman on the outside. Don't you want to be beautiful on the inside too? Wouldn't you rather people smile when they think of you, than shake with fear and loathing at the mention of your name?' I shrug. 'It's entirely up to you, Geneva. It's your life. You must live it in the way you want. But I do have people in my life who smile when they think of me and I smile when I think of them. So I really am leaving now so that I can be with them. I wish you well, Geneva. And I wish you happiness and love.

This time she doesn't say a word as I walk away.

Twenty-three

I tell my boss that I'm not sure what will happen regarding McBriar Properties and our software, but that the so-called meeting today had nothing to do with business.

I explain very briefly about Tori and Mack, that Mack was Geneva's ex, and about the properties Geneva wanted to acquire, but I don't go into any of the details and I don't tell him about the things she said regarding Gio.

He tells me he's happy with me walking away today and that Geneva sounds a little 'off' and perhaps we'd be best not to get involved with a company run by such people.

That's another thing I love about my boss. He's not ruled by money. Or by power. Yet he has plenty of both.

I call Katie and tell her everything that's happened and she asks me to meet her at Seascape Café as soon as I get back so that I can repeat it all to Tori and Mack. I want to

meet Gio but I know this is important and it's
better to do this first while it's still fresh in
my head, so I agree and when I hang up, I
write notes of everything that I can
remember Geneva said.

What I should have done first, was check
to see if I could get a flight. I have an open
ticket but that doesn't mean I can jump on
the first plane out. There has to be a seat
available. And there isn't.

The first flight I can get on is at 5.50 p.m.
and it's only 2.30 p.m. now.

I try to get another flight with a different
airline but there aren't any others available
when I check.

I'm stuck with the flight at 5.50 p.m.
which will get me to Heathrow at 7.15 p.m.
and from there it's a journey of an hour and
a half to home. Allowing for time to get off
the plane and out of the airport that means I
won't get to Seascape Café until around 9.15
p.m. and although Tori, Mack and Katie
won't mind, I do, because this also means I
won't be able to see Gio today.

Oh well. There is always tomorrow.

While I wait for my flight, I text Gio to
ask if he is free for a chat and when he says
he is, I call him.

I don't mean to tell him everything
Geneva said, but it all comes pouring out,
including the threat she made about my job

and about him being a 'criminal' and it's only when he goes silent, that I realise that was unwise.

'Gio? Are you still there?' I ask.

'Yes. I'm here. You're telling me Geneva is intending to tell your boss that you're in love with a criminal?'

Oh God. Did I tell him that too?

'Uh-huh.'

'But can't you simply deny it?'

There's a catch in his voice and I'm not sure if he's cross, nervous, or anxiously hopeful. I'm also not sure how to answer that. Geneva said that I am in love with Gio. How she knew that I have no idea but she is right. She also said that Gio is in love with me. I really hope she's right about that too but I have no way of knowing – unless he tells me it's true. I decide to err on the side of caution.

'I ... I suppose I could. But I don't think that part's a problem. What concerns me more is what might happen if she does spread rumours about you.'

'That's why I didn't want you to open that can of worms. No one has said anything to my face about what happened back then and it hasn't had an impact on my business. But if it were all to be brought up again, it might. I don't know how people will react.'

'But that's precisely why I want to tell the

truth! Then everyone will know it was me, not you.'

'And then your boss might fire you, Emma. Because thinking you may be in love with a criminal is one thing. You *being* a criminal, is something else entirely.'

He's right, I hadn't really thought about that.

'If that's what happens, I'll have to accept it.'

'No! You won't. That isn't going to happen because you are not going to say a word about it. Understand? You have worked hard and you've got a brilliant career. You are not risking that over a stupid incident fifteen years ago. And if Geneva carries out her threat, I'll take the blame.'

'Just as you did fifteen years ago. No, Gio. You also have your career to think about. You were innocent then. Of this at least. I'm not going to let you take the blame again and risk throwing away everything you've worked so hard for, just to save me. I think it's time we had that talk. I won't be home till late tonight but if you're free tomorrow I can come round at any time.'

'Let me think about it,' he says. 'We'll speak in the morning. Have a safe flight.'

And then he hangs up and I realise he didn't ask if I do love him. And neither did he confirm or deny whether he loves me.

I couldn't believe it when Geneva said he did, so it would be nice to know if she is right about that. She was right about most of the things she said. But not all of them. She may have been right about my feelings for Gio, but she may have been wrong about his feelings for me.

Twenty-four

It's Saturday night and Seascape Café is packed to the rafters when I arrive. There's also a couple of bands playing here tonight, so it's noisier than ever. When Tori became a partner and took over running the place, she retained the small team of staff that Lou and Dave had employed, and soon Katie will be joining her as a partner. They're all working here tonight because it was obvious it would be busy.

Tori sees me shortly after I arrive and she waves me through to the flat. Mack, Katie and Aaron, who is also helping out tonight as a favour, join us, and after Tori pours me a much-needed glass of wine, I tell them everything I had previously told Katie.

Tori and Mack are as horrified as Katie was when they hear of everything Geneva said and all her threats.

'Perhaps I need to try to speak to her,' Mack says, looking thoroughly miserable.

'I'm so sorry about all this.'

'It isn't your fault,' I say. 'This is about Geneva, not you.'

'But she wouldn't be doing any of this if it weren't for me.'

'Again, her fault, not yours.'

'Emma's right,' Tori says. 'You can't blame yourself for this.'

'And she's also right about all our friends sticking together and helping us out,' says Katie.

'Absolutely,' Aaron says. 'I know Meg and Rick will help, and probably Lucinda and Cody, too, once they know what's going on.'

'Portia will,' says Mack. 'I'm certain of that.'

'There you see!' I say. 'Geneva won't win, no matter what.'

'Why is she such a cow?' Tori queries.

'Her dad's a truly unpleasant guy,' says Mack, 'so I suspect she gets it from him. Her mum's not much better. She was a supermodel and she still thinks she's on the catwalk. From things Geneva let slip, she didn't have a happy childhood. Although she didn't like to talk about it, so I didn't get much out of her. But I do know that her mum didn't want kids and basically ignored her. Her dad doesn't love anyone as much as he loves McBriar Properties. He wanted a son to take over from him. He got Geneva instead.

She's been trying to prove herself to him since she was born but although I think he does care for her in his own way, he's never shown her love and affection. It's just business, business, business, and want, want, want, with him. I could empathise with her about being unloved by your family, of course, given the situation with my grandparents. But I had Vida who truly loves me. Geneva had no one. And, I suppose, looking back, I didn't treat her that well either. I never loved her and that's something I made clear from the start. It was just a convenient relationship as far as I was concerned. I thought she was happy with that, because she said that' what she wanted too, until recently, and then, of course, I walked away.

'I think you treated her well, given the situation,' I say. 'You never intended it to be any more than what it was. The problem is, I think, Geneva fell in love with you, whether she meant to or not. And she's a woman who has been brought up to get what she wants.'

'That doesn't excuse her behaviour,' Katie says.

'I'm not suggesting it does. I'm simply saying she's doing what she's been brought up to do. But it was really odd. As much as I hated her for her threats and for wanting to hurt us all, and seeming not to care one bit, something inside me told me she did care, and I felt sorry for her. I could be completely wrong, but I think if she got away from her dad and that business, and looked at her life and what she really wants it to be like, she might learn to become a nicer person. I told her today that she will attract more bees with honey than with vinegar and I also said she might want to try to be a nicer person. I swear that for one moment, it looked as though those words had hit home. As if she were wondering if that could be possible.' I shrug. 'Only time will tell, I suppose.'

We continue chatting for a while and then I realise how exhausted I am. It's been a hectic week and what with my early start, my flights, the car journeys, and my emotional rollercoaster of a day, I am absolutely shattered and struggling to keep my eyes open.

'We'd better get back to work,' Katie says, getting to her feet, and Tori and Mack follow suit, along with Aaron.

'I would offer to stay and help,' I say, 'but I really need my bed.'

'Call a cab on us,' Mack says. 'We don't want you walking home alone.'

'I'll be fine. I've got my overnight bag. I can whack any would-be assailants with that. Not that there are likely to be any would-be assailants in Norman Landing.'

'No!' Tori says emphatically. 'You're getting a cab.'

In all honesty, I probably would've done anyway. Not from fear of walking home alone, but simply because I do have my overnight bag and although it's on wheels, I'm tired and I don't want to drag it along behind me.

I don't have long to wait and I'm home and tucked up in bed no more than twenty minutes later.

I'm just about to drift off to sleep when I receive a text. It's from Gio and I sit upright, excited to read it. But the excitement quickly fades.

It says that he hopes I'm home safely and that he's got a very busy day tomorrow, so we may have to postpone our talk. It ends with the words, 'I'll text you if and when I'm free.'

Something inside me tells me not to expect to hear from him tomorrow.

Twenty-five

'Hi, Em! How's your week been without me?' Ben asks, looking brown and tanned and relaxed as he strolls into my office on Monday morning.

I'm not in the best of moods. I was right about Gio. I didn't hear from him on Sunday, so after hours of waiting and pacing and trying to pretend I wasn't constantly checking my phone to see if he had called or texted, I finally gave in and sent him a text.

'Hi. How's your day? Any free time looming on the horizon? Even ten minutes is fine.'

It was thirty minutes before I received a reply.

'Sorry. Not even one minute to spare today. Will be in touch in the week. Or next weekend.'

I almost threw my phone across the floor and then I came to my senses. It was my phone, not his, so that wasn't a good idea.

'Hi Ben,' I say, 'Have you been away?' I'm trying to lighten my own mood.

He grins at me and strolls over to one of the chairs on his side of my desk. He flops down into it and stretches out his legs.

'I've missed you, you know. I wasn't sure I would. But I did. Have you missed me?'

I'm surprised by that and there's something about him that tells me he's being serious and for once he isn't joking around.

'I have,' I say. And then I remember what's in my brief case. 'But not that much. I've had two very busy weekends. This Saturday I went up to see the McBriars. That was a complete waste of time, I think. I won't bore you with details now because you'll have plenty to do, but give me a shout if you hear from them. And there is another matter I want to discuss with you so let me know when you have some free time.'

He smiles. 'I've always got time for you, Em. You should know that by now. And, as it happens, I have some free time right this minute, so fire away.'

I look him in the eye. I have missed him. I've missed his smile, those gorgeous eyes, his laugh, his sense of humour.

'Okay,' I say. 'Don't judge me'

'Oooh. Sounds serious.'

'It is. Erm. I went on a dating website last week. Or the week before I suppose.' I shake my head to clear it but I'm not sure it works, as images of Gio come tumbling into my mind's eye. I fumble in my briefcase.

'A dating website?' he repeats, as if he's surprised. But I know he saw that print out so I tilt my head to the side and give him a look. He grins and shrugs his shoulders. 'Okay. I may have known about it. Please don't tell me you've found the love of your life. I couldn't bear it.'

I ignore that remark and continue to search my briefcase.

'I'm sure this is where I put the print outs I took. Ah yes. Here they are. Anyway, Ben. There was this guy on there, and he looks exactly like you.'

'Like me?' Now he is surprised.

I nod. 'Yes. Exactly like you. So I sent him a message, and it turns out he's a scammer. He wanted my phone number to ask me for money. At least that's what I assumed. Here're some screenshots I took before I deleted my account. You might want to look into it yourself, because either this guy does look exactly like you, or he's stolen your photo from somewhere.'

I toss the printouts towards him and he picks them up from my desk. He looks utterly bewildered.

'You're saying I'm on a dating website? You're on there too?'

'No. This guy is on there. I reported him. I was on there for a week or so but I've now deleted my account. Those should be self-explanatory.'

He flicks through the pages, his smile fading and the crease between his brows deepening. Eventually he stops and looks at me.

'Thanks. I'll definitely look into this. The thought of some guy pretending to be me and ripping off unsuspecting people, is bloody annoying. Or even if he's not pretending to be me and simply using my photo, that's just as bad.'

'Yeah. It is. Because if he cons someone and that person happens to live around here or sees you somewhere, they might think it's you and that could be all kinds of unpleasant.'

'That could be DEFCON1,' he says.

There are some things I haven't missed about Ben.

'It could certainly be serious. And there are some weirdos on dating sites. One of the men I met seems really nice but it turns out, not so much.'

I tell him about Tim, the flowers, and the messages.

'Blimey,' he says. 'Glad he's not my doctor.' And then he grins. 'He isn't, is he?'

'I doubt it. His practice is in Brighton.'

'Phew!' he says, still grinning.

'So how was your holiday?' I ask. 'Everything you hoped it would be?'

'Oddly enough, no. Honour is not the girl for me. A week on a secluded island really brings home to you the things that matter. What you do and don't like. What you want and don't want. And when you find yourself wishing that the girl you're with, was someone else. Well, suffice to say, Honour and I are no longer dating.'

'Oh, I'm sorry, Ben.'

He fixes me with an odd look. 'Are you sorry, Em?'

I'm not sure what he means and I hesitate for a second. 'Yes. I'm sorry it didn't work out.'

'What about you and the dating site? Find anyone you want to see again?'

I sigh. 'There was one guy I liked, but not enough to really bother arranging a second date with. And as it happens, he bumped into an old school friend later that day and now they're dating and he's deleted his account. He sent me a lovely message telling me all about it.'

'And you've deleted yours?'

I nod. 'Yes.'

'Any reason in particular?'

I clear my throat. 'Too much hassle. I simply can't be bothered. I'd rather be single.'

He doesn't respond right away but the look he is giving me is making my heart beat a little faster, so I shuffle some papers on my desk and pretend I'm working.

'Would you?' he asks.

'Sorry? Would I what?'

'Rather be single?'

I meet his gaze and our eyes lock. Heat is rising to my face and my palms are itching.

I shrug as nonchalantly as possible. 'Do I have a choice?'

'Yes,' he says. 'You do.' He continues to hold my gaze for a second or two longer, and then he beams at me, and pushes himself up from the chair. 'Think about it, Em, and I'll catch up with you later.' He gives me a little wave as he saunters from my office.

Has Ben just asked me out? Or am I imagining that? Perhaps all he's saying is that my future is in my own hands. But why then would he tell me to think about it and say he'll catch me later?

I find I think about little else all day.

Although every time my phone pings with a text, I keep hoping it might be Gio.

Twenty-six

I don't see Ben again all day, but then it is his first day back and he'll obviously be busy. I'm not sure if I'm disappointed or relieved, but each time someone passes my office, or taps on the open door, I look up half hoping to see Ben.

It's 5.30p.m. and I'm reading a particularly interesting report when I have the distinct feeling I'm being watched. I glance up from my desk, and Ben is leaning against the door frame, his arms crossed loosely in front of his chest and his legs crossed equally loosely at the ankles. There's a look in his eyes that tells me he has something serious on his mind, and when I give a little gasp of surprise, a smile spreads across his face that is so warm and inviting and completely irresistible.

'Thought about it?' he queries, tilting his head to the side a fraction.

'Thought about what?' I ask, the crackle

in my voice giving the game away, I'm sure.

His smile broadens and his eyes twinkle. 'Whether you want to be single? ... Or not?'

'I ... If someone asked me on a date, I might possibly say yes.' I try to sound casual. And fail.

'*Might* say yes?'

'It would depend who it is.'

'Ah. I see. Well ...' he pushes himself away from the doorframe and saunters towards my desk. 'I happen to know someone who has recently become single. I believe you might like him. He's a nice guy, I think.'

'Is he? And ... do you believe this ... nice guy might like me?'

'Oh I'm sure of it. Interested?'

'Possibly.'

He strolls round to my side of the desk and holds out his hand and despite the fact it's Ben standing there, I remember Gio holding out his hand to me and laughing hysterically when I put my hand in his.

'Want to come for a drink with me and discuss this further?' Ben says.

I grab my handbag with one hand, trying to do so as casually as I can while pretending my mind isn't doing cartwheels, and my head isn't about to explode, and my heart isn't yelling, 'What about Gio? What about Gio?'

I slip my hand in his and look him in the

eye.

'Sounds good. And I don't have anywhere else to be this evening.'

'So you're all mine then? For this evening.'

'I'm all yours. For this evening.'

He places a hand on my hip and moves in closer.

'And what about ... for another evening? And maybe more evenings after that?'

He's so close to me now that I can feel the warmth of his breath on my face, and smell the scent of his aftershave.

'I suppose that depends how this evening goes. But I don't have any firm plans at the moment.'

He leans in to kiss me and just before his lips touch me he says, 'I've been wanting to do this for a long time, Em.'

Twenty-seven

I have had a crush on Ben for about five years, ever since he joined the company, and during that time I have often wondered what it would be like to be in his arms and to kiss him. I had imagined it would be perfect. The reality is almost as good as I had imagined.

Almost.

There is only one tiny blip in this moment of bliss, and that tiny blip is Giovanni Russo.

Or more precisely, my own brain saying, 'Would Gio's kiss be like this? Would Gio hold me tighter? Would Gio–'

Shut up brain! I silently yell.

But Ben must've sensed something is not quite right as he eases away from me and looks me in the eye.

'Is something wrong, Em?'

I feel oddly guilty as if I've been unfaithful somehow. But I'm not sure to which one of them.

239

'No. I'm sorry. I've just ... there's been a lot going on lately and as wonderful as this is, I think it's taken me by surprise.'

'Me too,' he says. 'I like you, Em. I've always known that. Since the very first day I joined the company. We flirt, we joke, we get on well, but I thought we were just friends. Until ... until that day I saw that list of dates. Yes. I saw them. And don't look so surprised because you knew I had.'

I nod. 'That's true. I did. But why did that list make a difference?'

He shakes his head. 'Honestly? I don't know. All I know is that I spent the entire week on that beach in the Caribbean wondering who you were dating and whether you thought you'd found someone special. And then, just like that, I woke up one morning and I went for a swim and I wanted you to see how beautiful the place was. And I realised you were the one who is special. Special to me.' He makes a sort of strangled laugh. 'The last two days of the holiday were ... let's just say, difficult. When you call the woman you're with by someone else's name, it seems they're not that amused. And when you tell the woman you're with that you've realised you want to be with someone else, there is a chance they may get cross.'

'You didn't, did you? Really?'

He nods. 'I did. And talk about

DEFCON1, Em. Wow.' He shakes his head again and runs a hand through his hair. 'Not my wisest tactical decision. I should've waited until we got home.'

I don't mean to laugh but I can't help it. To think this man, this gorgeous man was thinking about me all week.

And better yet, this gorgeous man dumped his even more gorgeous girlfriend ... for me! I quite can't believe it.

'So what do you say, Em? Do you think we have a chance?'

'A chance?'

'Of making this work. I'm asking you out, Em. I'm asking you to be my girlfriend. I'm not aware of any company rules forbidding dating between members of staff, but if there are, we'll find a way around that.'

My body is screaming, 'Yes! Yes! Yes! but now my heart has joined my head and is saying, 'What about Gio? Didn't you want to date Gio? Don't you want to be Gio's girlfriend?'

'Em?' Ben is looking anxious. 'I ... I thought you liked me. Really liked me. Am I wrong?'

'No! You're right. I do. It's just that ... I don't know how to say this or even if I should because nothing is going to happen between us but ... Oh Ben! There is someone else I like too. And I need to make sure I can get him out of my head before I ... before we ... before...'

'I get the picture.' He sounds disappointed, but he doesn't sound cross. 'Before we take this any further. Before we sleep together, you mean, don't you?'

I nod. 'Yes. That's exactly what I mean.'

He smiles. 'That's okay. It's not the best news, I'll admit. But hey. All's fair in love and war, right? We'll take things slow.' He laughs. 'It's taken us five years already, so maybe not that slow, but we won't rush into anything. I won't select my best man or write my wedding vows, or anything like that. Is that okay?'

I laugh too, relieved that he's taking it so well. 'That's perfect. You're perfect.'

'Obviously not quite,' he says. 'But I'll batten down the hatches and prepare for war. Just promise me one thing, Em.'

'Anything.'

'Tell me if anything does happen between you and this other, lucky guy, okay?'

'I can definitely promise you that.'

He takes a deep breath. 'Right. Well, let's go and get that drink, shall we? I think I need one after that.'

He links my arm through his and we walk out of the office as a couple.

This is something I have dreamt of for years. Ben wants me to be his girlfriend.

It's so perfect.

So wonderful.

A dream come true.

Or it would be, if it wasn't for bloody Giovanni Russo.

Twenty-eight

I don't know what to do. One minute I'm dancing in the air with joy, the next I'm spiralling into the depths of depression.

Ben really likes me. I've wanted to be with him for years.

But I've wanted to be with Gio for even longer.

Last night with Ben was wonderful. We drank, we laughed, we talked, we held hands, we did everything a normal couple dating, would do. Except at the end of the evening, instead of continuing our date, as we both knew we wanted to, I went home in a cab, alone.

Neither of us trusted ourselves to part at my front door, and there was no way I could invite Ben in. Not until I was sure I only wanted to be with Ben, and no one else. We'd known one another too long to behave as if we'd just met and this was our first date, but I couldn't imagine sleeping with Ben and having thoughts of Gio in my head. That wasn't fair to either of us.

On Tuesday at work, my head is all over the place. Every time I see Ben I want to pull him into my office and kiss every inch of him. He tells me he feels exactly the same. Yet thoughts of Gio still keep niggling away at me.

There is only one way to resolve this. I need to see Gio and have that conversation with him again, and I also need to find out if there can ever be anything, romantically, between us. If he says no, I must find a way to dismiss him from my thoughts and concentrate exclusively on Ben. If he says, perhaps ... well, then I don't know. I suppose I'll have to decide which of the two I most want to be with. And which of the two I see my future with. There are no guarantees that any relationship will last, no matter how deeply a couple may feel for one another, but to start a relationship off wondering if you'd rather be with someone else, is definitely not a good place to start.

This is the sort of conversation that would be best held away from Gio's place of work.

I'm owed plenty of holiday and now that Ben is back, he can cover for me as I did for him. We haven't heard anything further from McBriar Properties so I have no idea what is happening there, but Ben has my number if Geneva rears her beautiful head.

My boss is both surprised and pleased when I ask for a few days off and tells me I can take as many as I want, on the understanding that I'll be at the end of the phone if there's an emergency.

I decide I'll take the rest of today and the remainder of the week. I've got some things I need to do at home and I know Tori and Mack, and now of course, Katie could use a hand. The closer it gets to the Seascape Café and Norman Landing Beach Concert, the more there seems to need to be done.

'I don't think I'm leaving you with any outstanding issues, workwise,' I tell Ben, 'other than McBriar Properties. But you've got my number, so call me if you need to, no matter when.'

'Roger that,' he says.

'And ... if you want to meet for a drink or whatever, I'm definitely okay with that. More than okay.'

He smiles oddly. 'Let's put that on hold, shall we? You've got a few things you need to sort out. Concentrate on doing that this week and this weekend and we'll start afresh next Monday. Hopefully, some of these issues will be resolved by then.'

'Are you ... are you saying you've changed your mind about dating me?'

'No. I'm saying I don't want you to feel conflicted this week. Take some time to think about us, and to think about what's getting in the way of that moving forward. I'll be here on Monday, waiting to pick up where we left off last night. Or … if you decide that you'd rather be with … this other guy, then you can tell me that on Monday. Okay?'

'Okay. Ben?'

'Yes?'

'Are you … are you really okay with this?'

He smiles wanly. 'Would I rather hear you say you love me madly and you don't want anyone else? Yes. Would I rather find out now if there is someone else? Also yes. Do I hope you choose me? Absolutely. Will we still be friends if you don't? Also absolutely. Stop worrying about me and go and sort this out. But … call me if you need me.'

'You're such a lovely guy, Ben.'

'Remember that this week. Now give me a kiss and get out of here, or I might change my mind and tie you to my desk.'

His kiss is so wonderful, so tender, so … perfect.

What am I doing? Why am I trying to ruin this?

But again my heart shouts, 'Gio!'

I drive home in a state of mild panic and rush inside to get changed. It's almost lunchtime but I can't eat. My stomach feels like a washing machine on a permanent spin cycle.

It's stiflingly hot again today. My office has air conditioning; my home does not, and the breeze outside is as warm as a tumble dryer, so I put on a pair of cherry pink, cotton shorts, a lime green T-shirt, and slip my now bare feet into white flip-flops. I suspect La Dolce Vita will be quiet on a Tuesday, even at lunchtime but I haven't been there on a week day so I won't know until I get there.

I smile at my reflection, not only because I'm pleased with how I look but also because I realise I'm wearing the colours of La Dolce Vita. Will Gio notice, I wonder?

I should have known he would, it's the first thing he comments on when I tap lightly on the open door of his cosy little office, although he does look astonished to see me. I asked Abbi if I could come straight through. I lied and told her Gio was expecting me. I've been there so often recently that it didn't occur to her to check, but I was worried Gio might make an excuse not to see me if she did.

'Emma!' There's a huge smile on his face and for a second it looks as if he's about to jump up and come and hug me, but he quickly resumes his seat, and the smile becomes sardonic. 'Are you applying for a job as a cheerleader?' He looks me up and down and his gaze lingers on my legs for an extra moment or two, and then something dawns on him and panic rushes across his face. 'It's Tuesday! What are you doing here on a Tuesday?'

'Aren't I welcome here on Tuesdays?'

'You're welcome any day. But why aren't you at work. Oh Christ, Emma! You ... you haven't lost your job, have you? She hasn't carried out her threat?'

'No. My job is exactly where I left it. Wait! I'll rephrase that. I haven't left it. I'm merely taking a few days holiday and I'm going to give Tori, Mack and Katie a hand. I haven't heard anything further from Geneva. I'm here to ask if you have any free time this week.'

The relief on his face is evident, until doubt creeps in once more.

'Free time? This week? Why?'

'Because you've been really helpful recently, and I want to repay you.'

I can hear the sigh from where I'm standing, but that's because I'm not that far from him.

'You bought me coffee and doughnuts the weekend before last. Oh, and let's not forget the skincare products. Those alone were payment enough. Have you noticed anything different?' He juts out his chin.

There's no trace of stubble; not even a

hint of it. Being completely clean shaven suits him. Unless...

'Erm. Are you saying it's made your facial hair fall out?'

He roars with laughter and shakes his head. 'No, Emma! But it has made shaving easier. And I think my skin feels softer. In an extremely macho, Ethan Hunt slash James Bond, way, of course.' A slight crease forms between his brows. 'Don't you like it?'

'Yes. Very much. It makes you look even more handsome than...' I've started so I might as well finish, '...than before. Erm. Anyway, I want to invite you to dinner. Or lunch. Or even breakfast.'

'Not afternoon tea?'

'If you like, yes.'

He throws me another sardonic look. 'And where would any of these delights take place?'

'At my house.'

His brows shoot up. 'At your house? Seriously?'

'What's wrong with my house?'

'Nothing, I suspect. Although as I've never been there, I could be wrong. But doesn't Katie live next door to you, with your neighbour Aaron?'

'She does. So what?'

'And you would be happy for her to see me arriving at your house and leaving a few hours later?'

'Yes.'

He looks me up and down once more and shakes his head.

'I'm free tonight. But I think this is a bad idea.'

'Why? Don't you think I can cook?'

He looks me in the eye and something tugs at the corner of his mouth. 'It's not your cooking I'm concerned about.'

'Then what?'

He quirks a brow. 'Do you really need to ask?'

Tingles are darting up and down my spine faster than a Formula One racing driver.

'Yes. What are you concerned about? Other than being seen by my sister.'

He casts his gaze down to his desk and keeps his eyes firmly fixed on something, although I'm not sure what. 'Let's not go there, Emma.'

'Fine. Is 7.00 p.m. good for you?'

'Yes.'

'Great. I'll see you later. Oh, and Gio. Don't be late.'

His head shoots up and a smile spreads across his mouth. 'As if I'd dare. I'll set an alarm on my watch and I'll be counting the hours until this evening.'

He's not the only one.

That was easier than I expected. I thought, after our last conversation and the fact that he's been avoiding me, he would instantly say no, or make several excuses, and I'd have to badger him to agree. But although he said he thinks it's a bad idea, he also looked quite keen to come. So I'm still not sure what to think. Does he like me or doesn't he? Hopefully, I'll find out the answer to that tonight.

From there, I walk to Seascape Café. Oddly enough, now that I know Gio will be coming for dinner tonight, I feel far more relaxed and I could eat lunch. If fact I realise I'm starving. I could have eaten at La Dolce Vita, but I didn't want to overstay my welcome, or give Gio time to think of an excuse not to join me for dinner.

His comment about Katie seeing him arrive at my house made me feel it might be wise to tell her, and as I know she is working here today because today is her first official day working as a partner in Seascape Café, I can deal with two things at once. I can have lunch. And I can tell Katie that Gio is coming to dinner.

To my surprise, Nan and Donald are also here.

'Hello,' I say. 'May I join you?'

Nan smiles up at me. 'Hello, sweetheart. Of course you may. You're looking very lovely and colourful today. And happy too. But why aren't you at work?'

'Thank you. I'm taking a few days off.'

'A few days off! Good gracious, are you ill?'

I laugh at that. 'No. It's simply a lovely day and I'm out enjoying the sunshine.'

'Same here,' says Nan.

'And to cheer Katie on, of course,' I add.

Donald laughs. 'Same here.'

I join them at the table and a couple of minutes later, Katie comes out to serve us.

'How are you feeling?' I ask.

'Like someone on their first day in a new job,' Katie says, laughing. 'But what are you doing here? It's Tuesday. Why aren't you at work? You don't look ill.'

'Thanks. I've got so much holiday owing to me and it's such a lovely day, not to mention your first day at the new job, so I've come to cheer you on.'

She looks at what I'm wearing. 'You're certainly dressed for it.'

I frown. 'Someone else just said that. Or something similar. I don't think I look like a cheerleader.'

Nan and Donald nod. 'Yes you do,' says Nan. 'But you also look lovely, as I said.'

'Hmm. Erm. Hypothetical question,' I say, fiddling with a set of condiments on the table. 'How would you all feel if someone you knew and liked very much, asked someone you didn't particularly like, to dinner? You wouldn't be there. It would just be the person you liked very much, and the person you didn't like. Having dinner. Together. As friends. With a view to perhaps, seeing if they could be more than friends. How would you feel?'

Nan narrows her eyes. 'I would feel as if the person I knew and liked very much, was telling me that they were going to be inviting someone I didn't like, to have dinner with them, regardless of what I actually thought about it.'

'Ah. Would you be upset?'

'I might. But I would remind myself that if the person I liked very much was inviting a person I didn't like, to have dinner with them, it would mean that the person I liked, liked the person I didn't like.' She suddenly bursts out laughing. 'Oh, for goodness sake, sweetheart. This is all so confusing. Why don't you simply come out and say what it is you want to say? And I think we all know what it is, don't we? You have asked the Russo boy to have dinner with you, haven't you?'

'How did you know?'

'Because I wasn't born yesterday. And besides, this is Norman Landing, sweetheart. People talk.'

Which is precisely what Gio is concerned about. Damn it.

'I have. Are you cross?'

'You've asked Giovanni to dinner!' Katie says. 'When?'

'When did I ask? Or when is he coming to dinner?'

'Both,' Katie says, ignoring my sarcasm.

I grin at her. 'I've just asked him. Before I came here. And he's coming to dinner tonight.'

'Well,' says Nan. 'There's a turn up for the books. And will this just be the one dinner? Or are you hoping there will be a breakfast, lunch, and more meals to follow?'

I smile sheepishly and shrug. 'I honestly don't know. Yes. I'm hoping, I think. But in a way, I'm not. And whether it will happen, isn't up to me. But in a way, it is. Erm. I can't believe this is all happening but there's something I need to tell you all. More than one thing actually. One of them depends on tonight. And I suppose the other one does, in a way.'

'Emma!' Katie says. 'You're usually always so precise and to the point. Stop waffling and say what it is you need to say.'

'Oh! Okay. Erm. Ben, the guy I like from work, has finished with his girlfriend and he's asked me out. We went out on a date last night, in fact.'

'Yay!' shrieks Katie. 'But wait. You just said you've invited Giovanni to dinner tonight and you want to date him. That is what you said, isn't it?'

'Yes. And that's the problem. I like them both. Really like them. Equally as much, I think. But I can't date two men at the same time, obviously. Not that I know yet whether Gio wants to date me. I think he does. I may be wrong. But I need to know, because until I do, I can't move things forward with Ben. And even if Gio does want to date me, he still might not. Because he's so worried about the past. More so thanks to Geneva. But I can't go on wondering if Gio wants to be with me or not and whether he would if there weren't things in his way. If you see what I mean.'

'No,' says Donald looking confused.

'I'm not sure I follow, entirely,' says Nan.

'Shall I explain it again?' I ask.

'Please don't,' says Katie. 'Tonight is pretty important then?'

'Extremely important. Because...' Katie is glowering at me so I stop.

'Then I hope you're not planning on wearing that.' She waves her hand up and down in the air, her fingers pointing to my colourful outfit.

'Of course I'm not. Although, I haven't even thought about what I will be wearing. I'll do that after lunch. The service here is appalling, isn't it? We've been here for at least ten minutes and the waitress hasn't even asked us what we want.'

Katie slaps me on the back with her menu.

I'm so relieved that, even though Katie, Nan and Donald are now aware I'll be having dinner with Gio tonight, and that I would like it to be more, they haven't given me the frosty reaction I was worried they might. In fact, other than Nan still calling him, 'the Russo boy', they don't seem that bothered. I must ask her to stop doing that. It makes him sound like the villain many people in this town, think he is, and if people hear Nan calling him that, it'll only confirm their suspicions.

We order three full English All Day breakfasts, because even though I'm cooking dinner tonight, all this anxiety has really made me hungry, but before Katie has a chance to leave our table, Tori comes rushing towards us.

'We've got the flyers for the first Seascape Café and Norman Landing Beach Concert! Look!' She's waving a bundle of them in the air and she puts four of them on our table. 'Aren't they beautiful? Later than we hoped they'd be, but well worth the wait, I think. Now we can replace the ones Mack and I hurriedly made and pinned up all over town.'

'Oh they're gorgeous,' Nan says, picking one up. 'But the ones you both made are lovely too.'

I also pick one up. 'They really are gorgeous. It's all definitely going ahead then? For the last weekend in July? And Lucinda Revere will be the headliner?'

I've had so many things on my mind recently, that the rapidly approaching, Seascape Café and Norman Landing Beach Concert had almost slipped my mind, although I wouldn't dare say that to Tori. I'd said that when the printed flyers she had ordered, arrived, I'd help deliver them door-to-door, so although they're late as far as Tori is concerned, when it comes to getting them delivered, it couldn't have been better timing as I now have a few days off.

Tori only took over the running of Seascape Café at the beginning of June, so to have arranged such a massive and spectacular event in such a short space of time is exceedingly impressive, not to mention, nothing short of a miracle.

She says she couldn't have done it without Mack. He's been handling everything with the local authority and all the health and safety professionals, including Norman Landing Fire and Rescue. It has taken a lot of coordinating and planning to ensure nothing slips through the net.

Of course, when someone like Lucinda Revere, the most popular solo artist on the planet, is going to be the star act, everyone is prepared to move mountains to make sure the event goes ahead. And the fact that Lucinda is performing here for free, as a favour to Meg, Aaron's sister, who happens to be dating Rick Price, the best friend of Lucinda's husband, Cody, is a dream come true for Tori. And for Mack.

'Yes,' Tori says, looking more excited than I have ever seen her. 'And her husband Cody, the famous, former Ski racer will be here, and he'll be signing copies of his new book. Nothing to do with singing, or music at all, really, apart from him being married to Lucinda, but it also means his fans will be here. And then of course there's Meg. She'll be here. I'm so thrilled she's famous in her own right now, as I know we all are. And of course, she's got a book of travel photographs coming out, so she'll have that for signature and for sale. Plus Rick Price, the famous winter sports photographer will be here.'

'Don't tell me,' I say, 'because I think I can guess. Rick has a book of his winter sports photographs coming out, and he'll also be signing and selling that at the concert.

Yes?'

'Okay smarty-pants.' Tori laughs, and so does everyone else. 'Yes. They'll all have books here. And it will mean all their fans will want to be here. So it won't just be music fans here that weekend. Everyone and their dog will want to come. Tickets are selling out fast. So if you want some, you had better place your order pretty smartish.'

'Of course we want some,' I say. 'We'll all be coming, won't we?'

Everyone nods in confirmation.

'And perhaps we should get one extra,' Nan says, 'in case someone we don't particularly like wants to accompany someone we do like.'

'Or possibly two extra if she's dating Ben as well,' says Katie.

'What?' says Tori, looking from Nan to Katie to me. 'Emma's dating someone? Who? What have I missed?'

'Emma is having dinner with Giovanni tonight,' Katie tells her. 'And she's hoping he'll want to date her. But ... she also went out on a date with Ben, her colleague from work, last night. She can't decide which one she prefers.'

'Wow!' says Tori. 'Talk about going from famine to feast. It seems you didn't need that online dating site after all. But out of Ben and Giovanni, which one are you leaning towards the most?'

'I ... I think, in a way, Gio. But Ben is so lovely too. I really don't know. I suppose you'd all prefer me to pick Ben.'

Nan smiles at me and she taps my hand. 'We'd prefer you to be truly happy, sweetheart, so whichever one of them makes you feel like that, is the one we'll all prefer.'

Her smile reminds me so much of Mum right now, that my heart aches, and I do feel a little guilty for a second or two.

Would Mum have been so easy going if she had been here today, and I had asked that question? Or would she, once again, have forbidden me from seeing Giovanni Russo?

I'll never know the answer, so it's pointless to beat myself up by asking the question.

What I do know, without a shadow of doubt, is that Mum, like Nan and everyone one else at the table right now, would have wanted me to be happy. And whether she agreed with my choices or not, now that I am an adult, she would have let me live my life, and make my own mistakes. But she would have offered her guidance, her honest opinion, and her whole-hearted love and support. Just as Nan and everyone is doing today, and will continue to do, I'm sure, no matter who I choose, because that's what people do when they really, truly love you.

Twenty-nine

When my doorbell rings at 6.30 p.m. I assume it must be Gio. I told him not to be late, but I'm slightly irritated that he is half an hour early, because I'm still wrapped in my bath towel, sitting at my dressing table, applying my make up. So when I hear my front door open and Katie yells from the hall, I'm surprised, but somewhat relieved.

'Where are you, Emma?'

'I'm in my bedroom, getting dressed. Gio's coming to dinner. Remember?'

'I know. But I must show you this.'

I can hear her footsteps thudding on the stairs as she races up them and a moment later she bursts into my bedroom. She's jumping up and down, and twisting to and fro, and waving her hands in the air.

'Either you're in pain,' I say, 'or something exciting has happened.'

She races towards me waving her left hand in front of my face and it's only then I notice the diamond ring sparkling up at me.

'Oh,' I say. 'You've had a manicure. How lovely.'

'A manicure!'

She waves her hand frantically and I must stop teasing her. I jump up and hug her, and then shriek, 'Congratulations! Aaron's proposed. When?'

'Today. Just now. He was going to wait until later, because we're having dinner at Alberto's this evening, to celebrate our six-month anniversary, but he said he was so excited that he simply couldn't wait until then. He brought me a glass of champagne, while I was getting ready, and then he said, "It's no good, Katie. I just can't wait any longer." And then he got down on one knee and popped the question. I know it doesn't sound that romantic. But it really was. Because he was so genuinely happy, and so excited. I'm glad he did it there, and not at the restaurant tonight, with everybody watching.'

I know she's telling the truth. She would have been embarrassed if he had proposed in such a public place.

'Right,' she says. 'I'll let you get on. I just had to come and tell you. And I've told Aaron we've got to pop in to Nan and Donald's before we go to the restaurant.'

'Good idea. If Nan discovers anyone

other than me, knew about this before her, she will throw a fit.'

Katie laughs. 'That's exactly what I told Aaron.'

She kisses me on the cheek, shrieks with excitement, and dashes back the way she came.

I'm so happy for her I want to burst into tears. But Gio will be here soon and I'm still not dressed. There's no way I'm going to cry and then have to reapply my make up.

I slip into the midnight blue, tightfitting, strapless dress I bought today, and when I look at my reflection in the mirror, even I like what I see. The hem is mid-thigh and with my matching, midnight blue sandals, my suntanned legs look pretty impressive.

I make my way downstairs, pour myself a courage boosting glass of wine, and wait for Gio to arrive.

I look at the clock every five minutes or so but as it turns 7 p.m. there's no sign of him. He'll be here any minute now, I'm sure.

He's still not here fifteen minutes later. Now I'm getting worried. I send him a text asking if he is running late, but I don't receive a reply. I call his phone and after ringing a few times, I get his voicemail. I leave a message and wait for him to call, but I still haven't heard from him fifteen minutes later.

Now I'm seriously worried. Gio would

never leave me waiting without letting me know why he is running late. And he would never ignore my messages and my calls.

Although he has been avoiding me lately.

And he did say this was not a good idea.

But even if he had changed his mind, and decided not to come, he would have let me know. I'm sure of that.

I search for the phone number of La Dolce Vita, but like his mobile, it rings and then goes to voicemail. I don't know what to do, or who to call. Has he had an accident? Has there been an emergency? Where can he possibly be?

I phone Alberto's, and Silvio answers.

'Have you seen or heard from Gio?' I ask, and he can obviously hear the panic in my voice.

'No. What is wrong?'

'I don't know, Silvio. All I know is that he's not here, and he's half an hour late. He hasn't answered my calls, or replied to my texts, and we both know that's not like him. I'm worried something may have happened to him. But I called La Dolce Vita and there's no reply there either. I don't know where he lives. I don't know what to do.'

'I will send someone to La Dolce Vita, and to his home, and I will let you know as soon as I have news. Do not worry, bella Emma. Perhaps he has just fallen asleep with his phone on silent.'

We both know that is something else Gio would never do, but as Silvio is trying to calm my nerves, I don't argue the point.

I pace the room, trying to think of what to do, and what might have happened, but all that does is increase my concern for Gio.

Being half an hour late might not seem that serious to some, but anyone who knows me is well aware it is to me. I hate it when people are late, and no one who knows me would ever leaving me waiting without letting me know why they were late and that they were okay. Gio definitely knows that, and he wouldn't do this to me. I know he wouldn't.

I call Nan and tell her what's happened.

'We're coming straight over,' she says. 'Don't worry, sweetheart. I'm sure there's a simple explanation, and he'll turn up with a smile, an apology, and a very good reason for causing you such concern.'

But he doesn't.

Katie calls to say that Silvio has told her and Aaron that Giovanni hasn't arrived at my house as expected.

'Do you want us to come home to be with you while you wait?' she asks, 'because we're fine with that if you do. Silvio said he'll let you and us know as soon as he has news.'

'No. You and Aaron stay. Enjoy your

celebration. Nan and Donald are on their way, so I won't be on my own. I'll call you if we need you.'

'Are you sure? We've only just arrived so it really isn't any bother.'

'Yes. Enjoy yourselves. No point in us all behaving like panic-stricken loonies.'

Nan and Donald arrive, and ten minutes later, so do Katie and Aaron.

'We can celebrate another day,' says Aaron, giving me a hug, right after Katie has done the same. 'We'd rather be here to make sure you're okay.'

'I thought about calling Ben,' I say. 'But I realised that might be inappropriate. I don't know where Gio could be, and I'm sure he wouldn't simply stand me up. I wish I knew what was happening.'

I don't have long to wait. A few minutes later Silvio calls. I put him on speaker so that everyone can hear, and he gives me the terrible news that I've been dreading.

Thirty

'A neighbour found him on his drive, lying beside his car,' Silvio says, 'and there was a wound to his head, but do not panic, he is alive. Unconscious, but alive. The neighbour called an ambulance and the paramedics have taken him to the hospital. We will join him there.'

'Oh my God! No! May I ... May I come too, please Silvio? Please! I ... I need to be sure he'll be okay.'

'Of course. I will come and pick you up. Be brave, bella Emma. Gio is fit and strong. He will pull through. We will all be praying for that.'

'No need to pick her up, Silvio,' Katie says. 'One of us will take her. We just need the details of the hospital and the ward. I assume it'll be Brighton. That's the closest.'

'It is,' says Silvio. 'We will know which ward when we arrive. We will see you there.'

Quite what happens after that I'm

honestly not sure. My mind is in a daze, my brain is in a fog, my legs feel like jelly and won't hold me up. Aaron has to virtually carry me. I'm shaking like a leaf and I'm crying uncontrollably.

All the way to the hospital I mumble, 'This can't be true. It can't be true. This must be a nightmare. When will I wake up?'

Donald is in the front seat of Aaron's car, while Nan and Katie are either side of me in the back, each holding one of my hands.

'Silvio is right about Giovanni being strong,' Katie says. 'He'll pull through. I'm sure he will.'

'What on earth could have happened to him?' asks Nan. 'Silvio said he was found by a neighbour, lying beside his car with a wound to his head. Did he fall? Was he mugged or something?'

'We'll know more once we get to the hospital,' Aaron says. 'The paramedics might have some idea and they will have passed that information on. If not, we'll have to wait until Giovanni himself can tell us.'

'Assuming he can,' I sob, terrified that he might not wake up, or that he's suffered some terrible injury that will result in him being unable to function properly. He might have lost his memory. He might have lost more than that. 'If I hadn't invited him to dinner tonight this wouldn't have happened. He would still be at La Dolce Vita, working.'

'That's ridiculous!' Katie snaps. 'You can't blame yourself for this.'

But I can and I do.

When we arrive at the hospital and go to the waiting room near the ICU which is where we're told they've taken him, Silvio and Alberto are already there and we all hug one another.

'Is there any news?' I ask.

Silvio shakes his head. 'Not yet. We must wait. Have faith.'

That's easy for him to say. This isn't his fault, it's mine.

All I can do is pace along the corridor and wait. Minutes seem like hours; an hour feels like a day, and when my bestie, Nuala appears, I'm not even sure where I am.

'What are you doing here?' I ask her after she comes over and gives me a massive hug.

'The hospital's short staffed as always. I'm covering nights in ICU this week. I've just seen your friend, Giovanni, and I thought you might be out here. I wanted you to know, the doctors are sure he'll be okay. They'll be out to talk to you very soon, but I didn't think they'd mind if I popped out and told you. And I don't really care if they do, as I'm leaving at the end of the week.'

'Oh, Nuala! Thank you. That is such a relief. I must tell the others. But do they know what happened?'

'He was hit with something, and I hate to be the one to tell you, but it looks like it was on purpose.'

I gasp at that. 'Someone attacked him, you mean? On his own driveway?'

Nuala nods. 'The police are here. A neighbour saw a man driving away in a hurry from the direction of Giovanni's house. But the neighbour didn't see Giovanni right away because he was hidden from sight by his own car and the shrubbery in his front garden, and the neighbour didn't think to look. Well you don't expect to find someone lying injured on their drive, do you? Sorry babe. That wasn't very tactful. It was the neighbour's dog who raised the alarm by rushing over and barking, and that's when the neighbour found Giovanni and immediately called an ambulance. I'd better get back. But don't you worry. He's in safe hands. I'll take extra special care of him. And don't tell anyone, but I'll keep you updated during the night via text.'

She winks at me and hurries off and I'm just about to tell the others when the doctor appears and says something very similar.

'We've still got another test to perform but things are looking very good. The MRI results are clear, other than a tiny section of swelling but that is reducing as we speak and we're expecting him to wake up any minute. If he does, then he should be fine. If he doesn't, we may need to do more tests. But from what we've seen so far, he should make a full recovery. He's incredibly lucky. If the blow had been a couple of inches lower, or more forceful, the news might not have been so good.'

Despite Nuala having already told me, my sigh of relief is audible. 'Can we see him?' I ask.

'Not yet. In an hour or two perhaps. Let's wait until he wakes up and we'll see where we go from there. Are you a relative?'

'No, I ... but he was coming to have dinner with me so it's my fault it happened.'

'I don't think you can blame yourself for someone else's actions,' the doctor says. 'But only family will be able to see him when he does wake up. Head injuries are always treated seriously and he was unconscious when he was brought in. He may be confused and agitated when he comes to, or he may have short term memory loss. It's best to keep him quiet and stable until we know exactly where we are with him. Are you his girlfriend?'

I shake my head. 'No. But ... I was hoping to be.'

Apparently, 'hoping to be' doesn't count. Silvio says that if anyone else asks, I should say I am related.

Despite what both Nuala and the doctor have said, waiting around is making me feel anxious once again. Short term memory loss was mentioned. What exactly does that mean? Is there a chance Gio won't remember who I am? Or who he is? Or how he feels? Will he remember what happened? Does he know who did this to him? Will he have forgotten? Was this a mugging; a random attack, or did someone deliberately target him? Is there a chance that person might try again?

I give myself a telling off. Now who's the one who has been watching too much TV?

But a little later, it doesn't seem quite so ludicrous. The police believe the attack on Gio was not a random incident. It was intentional. Due to the location of Gio's house, the length of his drive and other factors they have taken into consideration, including that it was light and that people were walking dogs, or working in their gardens when it happened, they believe the assailant is likely to have specifically targeted Gio.

Officers then take statements from Silvio and Alberto and also from me.

They ask if we know anyone who might want to harm Gio. Anyone who has a grudge against him, or anyone with whom he may have fallen out recently? They ask about girlfriends, and whether there have been any relationship issues with anyone recently. I am ridiculously pleased to hear that Gio doesn't have a girlfriend and that he hasn't been involved with anyone since his return to Norman Landing.

And when I am told by the officer taking my statement, that, according to 'others' I am the only person with whom Gio has seemed particularly close since his return, I am elated.

Until the officer asks me if I have any former boyfriends, or anyone else in my life, who might want to harm Gio. Or if I have met anyone recently, who has shown any unwanted attention in me, or behaved in a manner that has given me cause for concern, or if I know of someone who may see Gio as an obstacle, or competition of some sort.

And rightly or wrongly, not only does Tim from the dating site, pop into my head, but also, Ben.

I can't believe I can suspect Ben for even a second, of doing something as dreadful as this, but hadn't he said that all is fair in love and war?

No. It is insane. Ben would not do this. Ben is a nice guy. A lovely guy. Ben is ... supposed to be my boyfriend. Is it possible he wanted to remove his competition? He had actually used that word. I remember him saying it.

What on earth is wrong with me? I give myself a mental slap and try to pull myself together. Ben would not do this. He wouldn't. I am simply overwrought and tired and I'm letting my frenzied imagination run away with me.

But the officer says he will need to speak with Ben, and he will contact the dating site to obtain information regarding Tim.

And then it hits me that something terrible has happened to Gio and yet again, it may be because of me.

Thirty-one

The doctor who spoke with us earlier, tells us that Gio is now awake and the prognosis is good.

'Mr Russo is a little confused, and has no memory of the incident,' he says. So basically, Gio's present condition is precisely as the doctor had told us it might be. 'We expect him to make a full a recovery, but he will remain here for the next two days or until we are sure that is the case. Two visitors may now go in to see the patient, but only relatives, please. And do not stay too long. Five or ten minutes at the most. Mr Russo has sustained a head injury and the best thing for him now, is sleep.'

I might be imagining it but I'm sure the doctor looked pointedly at me when he said the bit about relatives only, as if to say, 'not you'. But as much as I'm dying to see Gio, I'm just relieved he's awake and that he will make a full recovery. That must be correct because the doctor has now said it twice.

'We will tell him you are here,' says Silvio, as he and Alberto follow the doctor.

'Thank you,' I say. 'And give him my ... best wishes for a speedy recovery.' I was going to say love, but after what's happened to him, possibly thanks to me, that's probably the last thing he wants from me.

Although, of course, the doctor has said Gio doesn't remember what happened. I'm not sure if that's good or bad for Gio. Knowing him, he will want to remember.

'That's such a relief,' Katie says. 'He'll be fine. No need to worry now. Why don't we take you home and you can get some sleep? They'll probably let you see him tomorrow.'

I shake my head. 'Thanks. But I need to stay for a while. You and Aaron go. And you and Donald, Nan. I'll be okay. I'll get a cab home later. Please go and get some rest. And thanks again for being here.'

They take a little more persuading, but when Silvio and Alberto return and say that Gio knew who they were and that he looks better than they expected, and I give a huge sigh of relief and smile happily, Katie and Aaron and Nan and Donald, eventually hug me and say they'll go. As do Silvio and Alberto, who also try to make me go and get some rest.

'Call if you need us,' Katie says.

'Don't stay too long, sweetheart,' says Nan.

'He was pleased that you are here,' says Silvio, 'but also cross. He says the last thing that he wants is for you to be worrying about him.'

I'm not sure whether to be pleased or not by that.

'I'll just stay until Nuala gives me another update,' I say. 'Then I promise I'll go home.'

A few minutes later, Nuala appears looking conspiratorial and takes my hand in hers, glancing around her as she hurries me into a room and tosses me a nurse's uniform.

'Put this on over your dress,' she says, 'and do exactly what I tell you, okay? I could get into serious trouble for this.' And then she grins. 'But who cares? You want to see him, right?'

'Of course. But not if it gets you into trouble. I keep doing that to Gio. I don't want to add you to the list.'

She shrugs. 'I gave you a rash. This is the least I can do.'

I laugh. 'I wouldn't shout about that. Especially not in a hospital.'

She grins at me as I smooth down the dress. 'You look good as a nurse. Come on. But we can't be long. We're going to pretend we're checking his blood pressure and his temperature. Just stand beside me and don't speak to anyone else.'

I follow her into the ICU and my heart is racing. Not just because I'm about to see Gio but also because I'm impersonating a medical professional. My heart races even faster as we stand beside his bed. His eyes are closed, there's a bandage on his head and several wires and electrodes are attached to various parts of his body. He looks so helpless and yet at the same time, so strong and utterly gorgeous.

I take his hand without thinking, and Gio opens his eyes and looks directly at me. He smiles as if he's pleased to see me and then his brows knit together as if he's unsure of who I am.

'How are you feeling, Mr Russo?' Nuala asks, standing close beside me so that she is, effectively, shielding me from sight.

'Erm. I'm feeling okay, thanks, or I thought I was, but I must be hallucinating. Or am I dreaming? Am I awake?' He doesn't take his eyes from me but he scans me from head to foot, or as far down as he can see from his almost prostrate position.

'You're awake, Mr Russo,' Nuala confirms.

'He doesn't know who I am,' I say. I lean closer. 'Gio. It's Emma. Please get well.'

'Emma?'

'Don't worry. You'll remember me soon. I hope.'

Nuala nudges my arm. 'We need to go.' And then she says to Gio. 'I'll be back in just a moment, Mr Russo. Try to get some rest.'

'Please call me Giovanni. Or Gio.' He's still looking at me.

I want to kiss him but instead I briefly squeeze his hand and then I hurry away, behind Nuala, glancing back over my shoulder as I reach the door. I'm both thrilled and concerned that he's still looking at me as we leave.

'At least he knows who he is,' says Nuala. 'I'll text you with updates. Now go home and get some sleep. You look awful.'

'Thanks. And thanks so much for that. You will call me if ... if he takes a turn for the worse, won't you?'

'Yes. But he won't. He'll be fine. I promise you.'

I remove the uniform, and Nuala smuggles me back towards the waiting room. From there I call a cab and I'm home half an hour later, feeling so much happier than I had when I'd left here all those hours ago.

I nearly jump out of my skin when I open the front door.

'Did you get to see him, sweetheart?'

'Nan? What are you doing here? Why aren't you at home?'

'I didn't want you to come home to an empty house. Donald's at home but I wanted to be here for you. So did you see him?'

'Yes. Nuala smuggled me in. And he did look better than I expected, just as Silvio and Alberto said he did for them. But ... I don't think he knew who I was.'

She pulls me into a hug. 'He will, sweetheart. He will. Just give it time. Now go and get ready for bed and I'll bring you up something to drink. Are you hungry?'

I shake my head. 'No. Just tired.'

I plod upstairs, clean my teeth, and change into my summer PJs of shorts and a sleeveless T-shirt and I get into bed.

All I can see is Gio's face, and his dark eyes staring up at me, and my heart bangs against my chest as I realise that, no matter what happens with Gio and me, even if that's nothing at all, I'm in love with him and there's not a thing I can do about it.

I could pretend I'm not, and continue seeing Ben, but would that be fair to anyone?

Ben!

Oh no! I had almost forgotten about Ben.

And the fact that the police will be asking him about Gio. They may have already done so.

I check my phone which I'd tossed onto the bedside table, but there's no text from Ben. I think there would have been if the police had turned up at his door. It's midnight, but he did say I could call him if I need to, and I should let him know about Gio and the police.

Although ... if he did do this to Gio...? Of course he didn't! Stop being stupid.

'How are you doing, sweetheart?' Nan asks, bringing me a mug of hot chocolate and perching on the edge of my bed.

'I'm not really sure, to be honest.' I smile at the cream on the top of the drink and the sprinkles of chocolate on the cream. 'It's the height of summer, Nan and you're bringing me hot chocolate and cream and chocolate shavings?'

'Yes.' She winks at me. 'And there's a drop or two of Bailey's in there so stop yapping and drink it. It'll make you feel better.'

I doubt that anything could do that at the moment. Apart from Gio texting me to tell me he's remembered who I am and he'll see me soon, but I do as she says, and she's right. A few moments later I do feel better.

'How much Bailey's did you put in this?'

She smiles and shakes her head at me. 'Never you mind. Now try to get some sleep. The last thing you want when you go to see Giovanni tomorrow is to be standing in front of him all puffy-eyed and washed out from lack of sleep.'

I'm pleased to note she is no longer calling him 'the Russo boy' and that also makes me feel slightly happier.

'Okay,' I say. 'But first, I must call Ben.'

'Surely that can wait?'

I shake my head and sigh. 'I don't think it can.' But then I realise I'm far too exhausted to have a conversation or to answer any questions he might have, and he deserves that much from me at the very least. 'Maybe you're right.'

She takes the empty mug from me and I slide beneath my duvet, and before I know it, I can feel myself drifting off to sleep.

Thirty-two

I slept well and I feel far happier this morning. Nuala sent me a few texts during the early hours saying Gio is improving, and I can't wait to see him later today.

But there's one thing I must do this morning that I'm not looking forward to at all.

I must phone Ben.

The smell of a cooked breakfast wafts up the stairs towards me and as if a rasher of bacon has hooked itself into my nose, I follow the tantalising aroma right to my kitchen table.

'Good morning, sweetheart,' Nan says. 'Did you sleep well. You look refreshed this morning.'

'I did thanks. You?'

'Not bad. It's surprising how much I missed Donald. It's strange how quickly we become accustomed to having someone special around and it's as if we're missing a limb or something when they're not there.'

'Oh, Nan. I'm sorry.'

'Phooey. It's not your fault. I wanted to be here for you and I'll be seeing him in an hour. He's popping round to pick me up later. What are your plans for the day? Apart from visiting a certain someone in the hospital, of course.'

She's smiling lovingly at me and I return an identical smile.

'I promised Tori I'd help deliver those flyers for the Seascape Café and Norman Landing Beach Concert, so I'll do some of those today. And I've got to call Ben. I should try to meet up with him, if possible, because telling someone you want to be with someone else, is not something that should be done over the phone.'

'You're telling Ben you want to be with someone else?'

I nod. 'Because I do, Nan. I really do. And even if he doesn't want to be with me, it's still not fair to Ben. I'd be constantly wondering and hoping and...' I shrug. 'It just wouldn't work. Are you ... are you disappointed with me?'

'Disappointed? Oh sweetheart! I could never be disappointed with you.'

'But ... you don't like Gio.'

She looks me directly in the eye. 'Don't give that another thought. As I told you yesterday, all I want is for you to be truly happy. If Giovanni is the one who makes you feel like that, that's all that matters. Besides, if you like him as much as you clearly do, he can't be all bad.'

'He's not even a little bit bad, Nan. He was when we first met, I accept that and so will he, but ... he didn't do what he was accused of, Nan. He honestly didn't. And once you know the truth, and you will because I'm going to tell you as soon as I've spoken to Gio, you'll actually think he is as wonderful as I think he is. I don't just like him, Nan. I love him!'

She searches my face for a second and then she smiles that lovely smile, so like Mum's I want to cry.

'If you love him, sweetheart, then we'll all love him too. Unless the man breaks your heart, in which case he'll need to go much farther than America to escape my wrath. But as I'm sure that won't happen, everything will be fine. Now eat your breakfast before it gets cold. It's going to be another scorching day today, I think.'

I hope Ben will take the news that I'm in love with Gio, as well as Nan seems to have.

I call him as soon as I finish breakfast.

'Hello, Em! This is a lovely surprise. How are you enjoying your holiday?'

'Hi, Ben. So far, not so much.'

I tell him all about what happened to Gio, including the fact that I had invited Gio to have dinner at my home. I tell him about the police, and that he will probably be receiving a call or a visit and I listen carefully to see if I can detect any giveaway signs of guilt. Not that I'm really expecting any. Ben wouldn't have attacked Gio. I'm almost certain of that.

'I'm sorry to hear about your friend,' he says. 'I really hope he does make a full and speedy recovery. As for the police, well, they're doing their job and I hope they catch whoever did this. But in case you have any doubts, it wasn't me, Em. I like you a lot, but I'm not the type of guy who goes around hitting his competition over the head. And I'm assuming Gio is my competition? He's the other guy you told me you liked, right?'

I swallow hard. 'Right. And of course you're not the type to do that. But they asked about boyfriends and such and I had to give them your name. Sorry.'

'It's not a problem. Don't worry. And luckily for me, I have an alibi for last night. I was with a bunch of mates from Uni celebrating the fact one of them has just got engaged.'

'Oh. My sister got engaged last night!' I had completely forgotten about that. I must get her and Aaron a card and a bottle of champagne today. I can get them a present when I find out if there's anything special they want.

It's so weird, but it seems as if everything happened so long ago, and the only thing that feels as if it's in the here and now, is Gio.

'What a small world! Oh. And I've got news for you. I was going to call you last night. Good thing I didn't what with everything you were dealing with. But I didn't because of my mate and the celebrations. Anyway, guess who I had a call from yesterday.'

'Erm. Not McBriar Properties, surely?'

'The very same. And from Geneva McBriar, herself. She told me they want to purchase our product and I'm meeting with the head of their IT department today. She said he'll be the one handling everything from hereon. She did mention a discount but she was happy with the usual. She seemed disappointed when I told her you were taking a few days off, but she asked me to give you a message. It's a bit weird but she said you'd understand it.'

'A message?' I tense instinctively. The last thing I need now is more hassle from Geneva McBriar.

'Yep. She told me to make a note so I didn't forget. Here it is. She said that she mulled over what you said and that she has decided to take your advice. She and her dad will be cancelling all their plans regarding Norman Landing, including those of a more personal nature, so don't expect to hear from her again. And she wishes you well, and hopes La Dolce Vita will make you happy. That's it. Weird huh?'

'Wow!' I can't believe Geneva McBriar not only listened to me, she actually took on board everything I said. 'Not weird, Ben. Just ... bloody amazing. Did she say anything else?'

'Nope. That was it.'

I laugh because I'm in a state of shock. Does this mean she's going to withdraw the claim against Mack, too? She did say she was cancelling all their plans, so maybe she is. I'll have to call Katie. Or I can just ask Tori and Mack when I go there today to help deliver the flyers.

'Are you okay, Em?' Ben asks.

'Yes.' I pull myself together. 'Although there is something I need to talk to you about, Ben.'

'There is? Why do I get the feeling we're at DEFCON1?'

'I'd rather do this face to face. Could we meet for lunch?'

He doesn't reply immediately and then he sighs and his voice is sad. 'We could. But if you're going to dump me, to be honest, I'd rather you did it now, over the phone. That way I won't have to look at your lovely face and think about how I won't get a chance to kiss you again.'

'Oh, Ben! I ... I really am sorry.'

'You've realised you can't get the other guy – Gio, out of your head, right? And I'm assuming that what happened to him last night has made you realise how much he means to you.'

'Yes.'

'Bad timing, huh?' Ben says. 'I should've asked you out years ago.'

'I should've told you how I felt about you long ago. But the truth is Ben, I still would've been in love with Gio. I might not have realised it the moment he came back, but it would've been so much worse if you and I had been in a long-term relationship. At least this way we can still be friends. We can be friends, can't we?'

'Yeah. I suppose you're right. And of course we can be friends. But it might take a couple of weeks for me to adjust, so bear with me.'

'I understand. And I really am truly sorry.'

'It's not your fault. These things happen. At least we weren't on a secluded island in the Caribbean.' He laughs.

'That's true. You mean a lot to me, Ben.

And you'll find someone who deserves a wonderful man like you.'

'Maybe I should try online dating? Oh that reminds me too. I signed on to the one that has my 'twin', and I also reported him. The company wrote back almost immediately saying he's now been removed and banned from their website. A lot's been happening here. A lot's been happening to you, too, of course. Sorry.'

'Please don't apologise. I'm glad that's sorted. It's a relief to know that no one on that site, at least, will be taken advantage of.'

'Em,' Ben says.

'Yes, Ben.'

'If you need me for anything, anything at all, just call me, okay. Day or night. Night or day. I don't mind. I'll do whatever I can to help. I hope ... Gio recovers soon. And I hope he feels the same way about you as I do about him. You deserve to be happy. I also hope he realises what a lucky guy he is.'

'Thanks, Ben. Have a good remainder of the week.'

'You too, Em. See you on Monday. Take care.'

I really appreciate Ben's kind words, and I'm sure he means everything he says. I do think I can call him if I need to, and I find that reassuring. And I also think he deserves to find someone special.

I wonder if he might be interested in Nuala. She's currently single.

'All okay?' Nan asks as I saunter back into the kitchen.

'I've just told Ben.'

'How did he take it?' She pours me a coffee from the pot she has made.

'He took it well. I wanted to meet but he said he'd rather do it over the phone. He's such a lovely guy, and if Gio tells me to get lost, I might've thrown away my chance of happiness with Ben.' I shrug. 'But I couldn't live a lie.'

'What's meant to be will be,' she says, as we hear a car on the drive. 'Speaking of which, that's Donald.'

She beams with sheer pleasure as she hurries to the door to let him in, and I pour him a cup of coffee.

When they leave, I nip out to Conqueror's Convenience Stores and buy Katie and Aaron a 'congratulations on your engagement' card and a bottle of champagne, and then I pop next door to give them the card and the bottle, and an update on everything that's happened.

Katie is a little sad for Ben. Although she does agree with Nan that all that matters is me being happy.

They're as astonished as I am about Geneva's message.

'I've got today off,' she says grinning. 'I know I only started yesterday but Tori insists Aaron and I celebrate our engagement properly. We're going to Seascape Café for champagne and cocktails this evening, so you must come. Nan and Donald will be there too, along with everyone else who knows us. Are you going to tell Tori about the message? Or wait and see if it does also mean Geneva will be dropping the claim against Mack?'

'I'm going to go there now and help deliver some of those flyers, so I'll decide when I get there. But I'm hoping they might have heard something already as the message was left yesterday.'

'She didn't mention it this morning when we chatted,' Katie says. 'Do you have time for a glass of champagne?'

'I always have time for a glass of champagne.'

Tori and Mack are celebrating when I arrive at Seascape Café around an hour later, having had two glasses of champagne, not one, with Katie and Aaron before I left their house.

'You won't believe what's happened!' Tori shrieks.

Mack pours me a glass of champagne without asking if I want one. This will be my third one today, but it is a celebration so it would be churlish to refuse. As if I'd even consider that for a second.

'Geneva and McBriar Properties have dropped their claim against Mack, and they're no longer interested in purchasing any of the properties in Norman Landing.'

'Yes! Wait. Did you know about this already? How?'

'Because Geneva left me a message with Ben and he told me what it was this morning. It didn't say she was dropping the claim but it did say she and her dad were cancelling all their plans regarding Norman Landing and not to expect to hear from her again.'

'Bloody hell,' says Tori. 'All that stuff you said to her on Saturday really must've hit home. We've called Katie and left a message.'

'I've just come from there. She and Aaron were dancing in the garden when I left. Her phone is probably on the kitchen worktop and she hasn't heard it. As for what I said to Geneva, it would seem so. Or maybe something else brought about the change of mind. We'll never know what goes on inside other people's heads.'

'Oh God!' says Tori. 'How's Giovanni? I meant to send you a text, or call you, but I thought you might still be asleep. Katie told us about it this morning. Oh, and she's engaged! Although she told us that last night before they went to Alberto's. Everything's happening at once, isn't it? Anyway, how is he?'

'Improving by the hour. Nuala is working in ICU this week and she's looking after him. She's texting me regularly with updates.' I smile. 'She even sent me a photo of them as I was on my way here. Look.' I bring the photo up on the screen and we all smile at the way Nuala is pretending to mop Gio's brow.

'Hmm,' says Tori, when I take a final look at the photo. 'I know she's your bestie, and we all think she's great, but you have told her how you feel about Giovanni, haven't you? Only it looks to me as if she might quite like him herself.'

Thirty-three

I'm sure Tori must be wrong, but the more I look at that photo, the more I wonder if she's right.

I can hardly concentrate on the flyers I'm delivering, but that might also have something to do with the fact I have drunk four glasses of champagne. I had another after Tori's comment about the photo.

I finally pop the last flyer through a letterbox and glance at my watch. I want to be at the hospital by 3.00 p.m. and I need to go home and shower again and change into something pretty.

The shower is refreshing and sobers me up a bit, and the pale pink and white striped, cotton sundress I put on is lovely and cool in this heat. I slip on a pair of pale pink sandals, the heels of which aren't too high. The last thing I need is to fall over at the hospital. Although I suppose that is the best place to fall if you're going to.

I get a cab and arrive at precisely 3.00 p.m. on the dot. Silvio is leaving as I arrive and we spend a few minutes chatting. He tells me Gio has improved so much they are thinking of moving him out of the ICU.

I'm smiling with delight as I walk towards his bed. Until I see Nuala is with him and they're grinning at one another. Tori is right. Nuala does like Gio. And it looks as if he might like her too.

I'm about to turn and walk away as I can't deal with this right now. I'm still a little woozy from the champagne and I could say something I'll regret. What was it Ben said about bad timing? Well, this certainly is.

'Emma! Hi!' It's Gio's voice and he sounds pleased to see me.

I take a deep breath and I march towards the bed.

'Hi babe,' Nuala says beaming at me. 'We were just talking about you.'

'Oh really? I thought you were working nights? What are you doing here?'

She quirks a brow and gives me an odd look.

'Overtime. I told you we're short staffed, and as I'm about to leave, I want to make as much money as I can while I have the chance.'

'You look lovely,' Gio says. 'You have no idea how pleased I am to see you.'

He's looking at me with such complete joy that my heart almost leaves my body. I see it as a cartoon heart with legs and arms and lips and it dives into Gio's chest, grabs his identical cartoon heart and with pouted lips our two hearts kiss.

'I thought I was losing my mind,' he continues, 'and it's such a relief to know I'm not. I saw you standing by my bed in a nurse's uniform in the early hours of this morning, and I thought I must be hallucinating. Nuala tells me I wasn't and that she smuggled you in to see me and you were dressed as a nurse.' He laughs and Nuala laughs with him.

That's why he's pleased to see me? Because he thought he was losing his mind?

I'm not laughing at all. 'I wanted to be sure you were okay, that's all. And as I'm not a relative, or a girlfriend, or anything, I wasn't allowed to visit you.'

'I'll leave you two to chat,' says Nuala, and then she glares at me. 'Come and find me before you leave. I want to have a word.'

'I won't be staying long. I have things to do.'

'Whatever. Find me.'

She smiles at Gio, he smiles back, and then he and I are alone.

'How are you?' I ask.

He's looking at me as if he's confused.

'Annoyed. Bored. Wishing I knew who did this so that I could repay the favour. How are you? You must've been furious with me for being late.' He's grinning now.

'I was. But then I was terrified. And when Silvio called to tell me...' I close my eyes as I remember that moment. 'I thought my world had come to an end.'

'Me too,' he says, and I realise I had said those words aloud. I hadn't meant to do that. 'I'm so sorry, Emma.'

I'm blushing and perspiring and feeling embarrassed.

'Nothing for you to apologise for. It wasn't your fault.' I cough. 'In fact, it seems, yet again it might be mine.'

'Yours? How?'

I tell him what the police have said and in doing so I realise I've also told him about me dating Ben. I'm feeling so flustered and woozy and ... odd that I'm not really thinking what I'm saying.

'You were dating Ben when you asked me to dinner? Is that why you asked me? To tell me your good news? To tell me you'd got your ... prince?'

'What? No. That isn't it at all.'

'But you were dating Ben when you asked?'

'Yes.'

'So if it wasn't to tell me that, why was it?

Oh. I know. To tell me yet again that you want to come clean about the past.'

'Well, yes, but–'

'Okay. Fine. You win. You want everyone to know? Then tell them. And perhaps you're right. Perhaps it is time.

'Please don't be cross. I want to tell them to clear your name. So that no one will think badly of you.'

'When will you understand it's not my name that matters. It's yours. I don't care what people think of me. Apart from you. The rest of it doesn't matter a jot to me. It was fifteen years ago, Emma. Fifteen years. A lot has happened since then. The only person I ever wanted to know the truth, is dead. And that was Nonna. And I think, deep down, she knew. No one else matters. I've put what happened then, behind me. Why can't you?'

'Because I ruined your life, Gio!'

He laughs suddenly. 'You did not. If anything, you saved my life. Can't you see that?'

'Saved it? How? Oh, by getting you away from Norman Landing, you mean. And getting away from me. Because I was the one who got you into trouble.'

He quirks a brow and grins. 'I'm glad that was your line and not mine.'

'What? Oh. Erm. Yes.'

I cast my eyes down to the sheets on his

bed and I'm blushing like crazy. If only he had got me into *that* sort of trouble. I wouldn't have minded one bit. In fact, I'd have been the happiest teenaged-mum on the planet. But we never even kissed.

'That wasn't exactly what I meant, Emma. Look at me.' I look at him and there's something in his eyes that sends my heart soaring. 'You were only fifteen. I was nineteen. I may have been a bit of a chancer and on my way to a life of crime but even then I had a few morals. I liked you a lot and I was well aware of how much you liked me, in those days anyway, but I would never have taken advantage of you like that. Yes I was glad to get away from Norman Landing, and yes, I was glad to get away from you. But not for the reason you think. I was falling in love with you, Emma, and that couldn't happen. You deserved better than the life I could've hoped to have given you then.'

'What? You ... you were falling in love with me?' I can't believe I'm hearing this and when he nods, I want to kiss him. But I don't.

'Yes. But you were too good for me. That's why I took the blame. I thought I'd go to prison or something, and I'd probably end up like my dad, but you'd find someone else and forget me. It broke my heart when Reverend Wright told Nonna I had to be sent away, but it also answered my prayers. I thought you'd definitely forget me if I was in America. You'd have the life you deserved. A good life with a decent man. I didn't even consider then that I'd been given the chance of a lifetime. That's how you saved my life, Emma. I would've ended up like Dad if I'd stayed. Going to the States meant I had a fresh start. I worked hard. I changed my ways. I was determined to become the man I wanted to be. The sort of man a woman could be proud to share her life with.'

I'm trying to take in what he's said, but I'm still a little woozy, and when a doctor comes over and suggests that Gio needs his rest, I wonder if Gio is a little woozy too, or to use the medical term in his case, concussed.

Is he aware of what he's saying?

'I think the doctor wants me to leave,' I say, when Gio doesn't continue.

'I think he does,' he agrees. 'And he's probably right. But Emma?'

'Yes, Gio?'

'If you think this is the bump on my head, talking, you're wrong. I mean every word I've just said.'

'Every word?'

'Yes. Are you ... are you still dating Ben?'

'No. And we only went out for one evening. Nothing happened, apart from a kiss or two. But we're still friends. And we work together, of course.'

'A kiss or two? Lucky guy.'

'Do you mean you think he's lucky, or are you being sarcastic? Sometimes I can't tell.'

He smiles. 'He's lucky. Very, very lucky.'

'But you keep saying that it wouldn't work between us. That too many people know about the past. I don't get it. Are you now saying you don't care about the past? If you mean that, you could be lucky too. Very, very, very lucky.'

His eyes light up and I almost swoon at his dazzling smile.

'I've never cared about the past in respect of myself, Emma. I simply care about how it will affect you. A hugely successful, well respected business woman, dating a former – although never charged or convicted – petty criminal. I don't think that would go down well. As Geneva herself made clear.'

'Oh. You can forget about Geneva. She's had ... an epiphany. A complete change of heart, it seems.'

'She has?'

'Yes. But before they throw me out, let me get this straight. Are you saying that the only reason you think it wouldn't work between us is because of what people will think about me dating you, and that I might decide that their opinions matter, and I'll want to end things with you?'

'Yes. I think so. My head is getting fuzzy.'

'Mine is too. So I'll just say this. I don't care what anyone thinks, Gio. All I care about is you. Get some rest. I'll see you later.'

I'm so happy I could sing. But it's probably inappropriate, so I don't.

'Oi!'

I'd forgotten I was supposed to find Nuala. She doesn't sound happy.

'Hi Nuala.'

'Don't give me, "Hi, Nuala". What was that about just now?'

I consider lying but what's the point.

'I was jealous. I saw you laughing together and I thought you might like one another. I'm sorry. Plus, I'm a little tipsy.'

'You're bloody crazy. That's what you are. That man is head over heels in love with you. All he's talked about is you. Can't you see the way he looks at you?'

'Yes. I think so. But he's always teased me and still does, so sometimes I don't know if he's serious or not. He has just said the most wonderful things though. Oh. That's not because he's been hit on the head is it? He will remember what he's said won't he?'

'You're the one who needs to be hit on the head. It might knock some sense into you.' She rolls her eyes at me. 'Stop wondering about whether he's teasing you or not, because even teasing is a sign of affection, you know, and just tell him how you feel. In one sentence, preferably. Two at the most. Just say, 'I love you Gio. Do you love me?' And when he says yes. And he will. Because he does. Just kiss him! Okay?'

'Okay. I'll do that. I'll see you later. And Nuala.'

'Yes?'

'I love you too.'

'And I love you. See how easy it is? But don't even think about kissing me. Now go. I'm a busy woman and I've got important things to do. Where the hell did I put that bed pan?'

Thirty-four

Life sometimes sends mixed messages.

I'm so happy I'm not even looking where I'm going because all I can think about is Gio.

The blaring horn startles me and I quickly step out of the way of the oncoming car. That was a little close for comfort. I need to be more careful.

I'm supposed to be waiting for a cab which I think should be somewhere close by. The only vehicle I can see approaching is a large white van.

My head is feeling woozy, and the sun is blaring down, so I close my eyes and think about what I'll say to Gio this evening. Nuala is right. I should just tell him straight out. No talking about the past and how we felt then, no wondering what the future might hold. Simply saying how we feel right now.

And just when I think that, after all these years, I may finally be in Gio's arms by this evening – even if it is in a hospital, surrounded by other patients, and nurses, and doctors (I'll take whatever I can get) I find myself wrapped in someone else's arms. And they are the last person on the planet whose arms I would ever want to be in.

'I told you you'd be sorry,' Tim snarls. I briefly glimpse the back doors of a white van, one of which is open, as he unceremoniously bundles me inside, and whatever is on the cloth he is holding over my mouth, sends me into a state of stupefaction.

Thirty-five

I am in a giant washing machine. No. A giant tumble dryer. There's no water in here with me.

But what am I doing in a giant tumble dryer?

Pain shoots through my body as I'm tossed from one side to the other. I'm also sliding forwards and back. I hit my head and then I stub my toe. I hit my left arm and then my right leg.

Gradually the fog by which I am surrounded starts to lift. It's not a tumble dryer; it's a van.

Memory crashes down on me.

A van Tim threw me into.

Where is he taking me? Am I going to die?

Are those sirens I hear? Are those car horns blaring?

I try to move my arms and legs but I can see that they are tied.

And then I thud against the side wall of the van and this time I don't roll back.

I roll over and over and over until I lose consciousness for the second time today.

Thirty-six

I can't seem to stay awake. Every time I open my eyes, I want to close them again. I don't know how long this goes on for but it seems to be for days.

And now, each time I open my eyes, Gio is by my bedside. Sometimes Nan is with him, and sometimes Donald is too, and Katie and Aaron, and Tori and Mack. Nuala is there, and so is Mo. I really must make an effort to see my two besties more often. Even Ben is there a few times. And I'm sure my boss is there once or twice.

Why do they keep visiting me in my bedroom when I am trying to sleep?

If this is a dream it's an awfully long one. But it must be a dream because it's dark.

Except it's not. Not in front of me and not when I open my eyes. When I open my eyes it's often bright. Really bright. Too bright. Why won't they turn off the light when they leave?

When will it be morning?

Why doesn't this smell like my bedroom? It smells of disinfectant. It sometimes smells of pee.

Why do they keep saying my name? Repeating it over and over again.

Why do they keep playing music? At least it's all my favourites. Songs that Mum and I would dance to in the kitchen in our old home. And Katie and Nan would join us and we'd all hold hands and sing along with the words.

Is that Lucinda Revere's voice? Is she here in my bedroom? No wonder she's so popular. I can't wait to see her at the first Seascape Café and Norman Landing Beach Concert.

And is that Meg, and her boyfriend Rick? And Lucinda's husband, Cody? Why are they here? I'll be seeing them all at the Beach Concert.

Why are Nan and Katie often crying? Surely they're both happy? Nan's just moved in with Donald. Katie's just got engaged.

And why does Gio look so sad? Sometimes cross. Sometimes frustrated as he paces the room.

Surely I will wake up soon? I can't stay in bed forever. I've got a date with Gio. I'm sure I heard him say that. It was the last time I opened my eyes.

'Stay with me, Emma,' he said. 'We'll have a date at the end of the pier. You can eat Bacio and Pistacchio ice cream for dessert and I'll have bombolini. Emma? Emma!'

What is the man thinking? Bombolini? On a date? Our first real date?

'Bombolini?' I say, although my throat feels dry and sore and it feels as if I'm speaking through a straw. I shake my head as I open my eyes. 'No way. Not on our first date.'

'Emma! Emma, can you hear me?'

'Of course, Gio. But why are you crying?' I look around the room. 'Why is everyone crying?'

Or are they laughing? It's difficult to tell.

But when I look at Gio again, his smile is dazzling, despite the tears in his eyes.

Thirty-seven

'I still can't believe I was in a coma for four weeks,' I say. 'Although I suppose, as I did occasionally open my eyes, I was drifting in and out a few times.'

'I still can't believe you're a medical miracle,' says Katie. 'You never do anything by halves.'

Tori tuts loudly. 'I still can't believe you were not only late for the first ever Seascape Café and Norman Landing Beach Concert, you damn well missed it! I'll never let you live that down you know. You'd better not be late to the next one at the end of August. Especially as Lucinda is coming back especially for you!'

'I won't be late. I promise.'

Katie is at my house, helping me put on my make-up for a date at the end of the Pier tonight, and Tori is at Seascape Café on a video call with us.

'I can't believe I was so wrong about

313

Giovanni,' says Nan, bringing us a tray with three mugs of tea.

I take a sip of mine. It tastes like nectar. I look in the mirror and smile. I can't believe that, having kept my secret for fifteen years, Gio and I sat here in this very room less than one week ago and, surrounded by everyone who matters to us both, including Silvio and Alberto, we told the truth of what happened that day.

'I was stealing here and there,' Gio admitted. 'Nonna knew and she always paid for the little things I stole. When Emma started hanging out with all of us, I pretended I stole bigger things, more expensive things, basically just to impress her. I could see she hung on my every word and no one had ever given me that much time or attention. But then I said I was going to stop and get myself a job. Which I did. At the little ice cream parlour on the pier that was owned by another Italian family, as you probably recall.'

'I started stealing,' I said, and everyone gasped as I knew they would, shortly before Gio stopped. I wanted to show him I wasn't scared of anything. But mainly, and I hate to say this, I wanted pretty things, lovely clothes, jewellery, all the things I thought would make him like me more, see me as a woman and not a girl. But also I wanted those things because we were so poor at the time. Me stealing, was one of the reasons Gio stopped. He didn't want that life for me. I was too silly then to realise. I went into Holy Trinity Church one day and Reverend Wright had left the door to the vestry open. There was a big box on his desk and I knew that was where the funds for the repair of the church were kept. Why he kept it in cash, is beyond me, but he did. I don't know why I did it, but I stole the box and all the money it contained. And it was a lot. I told Gio. He was furious and he said we had to take it back. So we did.'

'Unfortunately Reverend Wright saw me in the vestry, just as I was about to put the box on his desk where Emma told me she got it from. He saw me through the window from outside. I told Emma to run into the church which she did and she thought I was right behind her, but he came in via a door neither of us knew was there. He naturally thought I was stealing it. He called Nonna, not the police, thank God, and gave me the whipping of my life, with Nonna's blessing. I vowed I would never steal again, and I haven't. The Reverend said he wouldn't contact the police, and Nonna said she was sending me away to America to live with distant relatives. That was the best thing she ever did for me. And I also thank Emma, because without that happening I would've ended up just like my dad, and would be in prison now. Instead, I have my own business and am able to give to charities to support kids like I was, back then.'

'Mum saw me running out of the church and took me home because she said I shouldn't have been there. She had no idea what was happening inside. I let Gio take the blame because I was too scared to tell the truth, and because Gio insisted I didn't tell anyone it was me. Mum and everyone heard the gossip about Gio stealing from the church and forbade us from seeing him. I did confess to Reverend Wright but he wouldn't believe me and he told me never to speak of it again because it would bring terrible shame on Mum and you and Katie, Nan. So I didn't. Soon after that, Gio left. I never stole again either.'

'And no one else knew the truth until today?' Nan asked in disbelief.

'No one. Are you ashamed? Are you disappointed in me now?'

'No, sweetheart. Surprised, yes. Sad that you thought you couldn't speak to us about this. But never disappointed. Never ashamed. We have all done stupid things in our past. Some more stupid than others. You saw the errors of your ways and stopped. That is good enough for me.

It took a few days for everything to sink

in, but since then, no one has treated either Gio or me any differently.

'But are you sure you're well enough for all this excitement?' Nan asks me now, as Katie finishes my make up.

'Absolutely! I slept for four weeks, and I've rested here at home for two more. Today the doctor pronounced me well enough to resume normal life.' I wink at Katie. 'And also said I'm a medical miracle.'

'There has never been anything normal about your life,' says Tori. 'But there have been one or two miracles around here of late. Not necessarily medical, but miracles all the same.'

She's right about that.

Since waking up from my coma, I discovered that the van I was in and that Tim was driving was being pursued by police. Someone had seen me being abducted and had dialled the emergency services. During the high-speed chase, the front wheel of the van hit a traffic island in the middle of the road, and the van flipped over and rolled down an embankment onto a railway track. Aaron was the firefighter who cut me free from the crumpled wreckage, while other members of the crew together with the police, managed to get the approaching train stopped before it got too close.

'You're right,' I say. 'The crash could

have killed me, but it didn't. The train could've hit the van, but it didn't. I could've sustained life altering injuries, but I didn't. And so could Gio, when Tim attacked him. But Gio, like me, has made a full and complete recovery.'

'And Tim is in prison where he belongs,' says Katie.

'And that Donald's children have finally decided that perhaps they do want their dad in their lives, although we'll have to see how they behave from hereon,' says Nan, 'if we're talking about miracles.'

'Yeah,' says Tori, 'All of that. And also that Mack's grandfather dropped dead. I know that's not a miracle and perhaps it's a little sad, but the man was horrible. The miracle is that he changed his will before he died and left everything split equally between Vida and Mack, and that Mack's mum's own engagement ring has been with the old git for all these years and only now has been passed on to its rightful owner. And, I think it may very soon have a new owner, namely me. And that *is* a bloody miracle.'

'Has Mack proposed?' I ask. I hadn't heard about that. Or about the return of the ring. Or the will. I had heard the old man had died.

'No. But I think he will. He keeps saying that after what happened to you and Gio, we should live each day as if it's our last and not put things off just because some people may think it's too soon.'

'That does sound promising,' I say. 'But not as promising as my date is going to be. I can't wait to meet Gio at the end of the pier tonight.'

Thirty-eight

Gio gives me a dazzling smile as I walk towards him. He looks so handsome in a pair of midnight blue trousers, a matching leather belt and matching shoes, together with a pale blue cotton shirt, the top two buttons of which are open.

I'm wearing that midnight blue dress I wore on our fateful 'date' the night Tim decided to follow Gio from La Dolce Vita.

Tim had been stalking me, it seems, and had seen me and Gio together on various occasions. Although Tim never came to my house, thankfully, but after I sent that message about someone from my past, Tim decided it must be Gio, and on that particular day, had followed Gio home. Someone was in the front garden next door when Gio arrived, so Tim waited. At least all this is what Tim has confessed to the police. When Gio reappeared and was about to get into his car to drive to my house, Tim hit him with the branch of a tree that was lying on the ground. Tim said it was a spontaneous decision and wasn't planned. I'm not sure I believe him.

But I don't want to think about Tim now. Gio is smiling at me and I know that tonight is the start of many wonderful nights to come. Because Gio has told me he loves me and I have told Gio I love him.

'You look breathtaking' he says, as he pulls out a chair for me at a table he has moved to the end of the pier, a few feet from the rear entrance to La Dolce Vita.

'So do you,' I say, as I take my seat.

He softly brushes my bare shoulder with his fingers, and tingles race all over my body.

'Are you hungry?' he asks.

'Not especially,' I say. 'At least, not for food. I hope you haven't gone to too much trouble.'

He grins at me and shakes his head. 'No. I haven't. But I have prepared something special. Excuse me and I'll get it.'

He isn't gone long but I breathe in the salty sea air. It's warm. But then again it is the beginning of August, so it should be.

If I'm completely honest, all I want tonight is Gio, not food.

We've kissed many times during the last two weeks and each time has been so wonderful, and better than the first, and that one was mind-blowingly good. But he's been holding back, because, until today, neither of us was sure if I was well enough for anything too ... let's say, intense or energetic. Now that I've been given the all-clear, I'm ready for everything he has to offer. And I am absolutely certain that he has A LOT to offer.

'Here it is,' he says, and my heart swells in my chest as he places a heart-shaped plate in front of me. 'But don't panic. I'm not proposing on our first date. This is just to show you how I feel. Because I love you, Emma Barr. And I've loved you for more than fifteen years.'

On the plate sit two intricately shaped and entwined, ice cream hearts. One of Bacio and one of Pistacchio and on the hearts are our names, also entwined. Around the hearts, using melted chocolate, he has written, Emma and Gio, Forever. La Dolce Vita. And right in the centre of the hearts are two large chocolate wedding rings. One large one for a man and a smaller one for a woman.

I can't believe my eyes. 'This is so beautiful, Gio.' And when I look at him, he gets down on one knee and produces a pastry box. I open it and inside there are two tiny bombolinis. I have never seen doughnuts as small as these.

'I was determined to have bombolinis on our first real date,' he says grinning at me.

'I thought you weren't proposing?' I say,

really hoping he is.

'Do you want me to propose? I will if you say yes.'

'Say yes to you proposing? Or yes to us getting engaged?'

'Yes to both.'

'Then I say, Yes. And Yes. And Yes.'

'That's three yesses.'

'I know. The other yes is to anything else you might have in mind.'

His eyes light up and he beams at me.

'I have several things in mind. But shall we begin with will you marry me?'

'Yes, I think we should. And Yes, Gio, I will marry you.'

Now he pulls from his trouser pocket a velvet box and opens it to reveal a stunningly beautiful eternity ring encircled with heart-shaped diamonds.

'Oh Gio! This is breathtaking.'

'There are fifteen diamonds,' he says, 'one for each of the fifteen years we were apart.' He slides the ring gently onto my wedding finger and it fits perfectly.

'You're such a romantic, Gio. This is wonderful. Oh, but what is in the tiny bombolinis then?'

He shrugs. 'They're just tiny bombolinis. One with *Nutella* and one with crema pasticciera. I thought they would make you smile.'

I place a hand on each side of his face as he's kneeling in front of me.

'You make me smile, Giovanni Russo. You make me happier than I thought I could ever be. You make my heart sing and my entire body, tingle. I love you with all my heart.'

'And you have made me the man that I am, Emma Barr. I wanted to be good enough for you. I wanted to come back to Norman Landing one day, and make you fall in love with me and ask you to be my wife.'

'Gio. You were always good enough for me. And I've always loved you, even when I wasn't sure I'd ever see you again. Being your wife will be a dream come true. Now please kiss me, Gio. And now that I have the all-clear, we can do anything else we can think of.'

This time when he kisses me, he doesn't hold back.

And neither do I.

We've been apart for fifteen years.

And that's a lot of time to make up for.

Coming soon

Visit www.emilyharvale.com to see
what's coming next.

Plus, sign up for Emily's newsletter, or join
her Facebook group, for all the latest news
about her books.

Stay in touch with
Emily Harvale

Sign up for Emily's newsletter to find out about book releases, see covers, help name characters or pick book titles, enter giveaways and lots more.

Go to **www.emilyharvale.com** to sign up.

Or join her Facebook group for all of the above and to chat with Emily and others about her books:

www.emilyharvale.com/FacebookGroup

Alternatively, say 'Hello' on social media:

 @EmilyHarvaleWriter

 @EmilyHarvale

 @EmilyHarvale

A Note from Emily

Thank you for reading this book. I really hope it brought a smile to your face. If so, I'd love it if you'd leave a short review on Amazon, or even just a rating.
And, maybe, tell your friends, or mention it on social media.

A little piece of my heart goes into all my books. I can't wait to bring you more stories that I hope will capture your heart, mind and imagination, allowing you to escape into a world of romance in some enticingly beautiful settings.

To see my books, or to sign up for my newsletter, please visit my website. The link is on the previous page.

I love chatting to readers, so pop over to Facebook or Instagram and say, 'Hello'. Or better yet, there's my lovely Facebook group for the latest book news, chats and general book-related fun. Again, you'll find details on the previous page.

Also by Emily Harvale

The Golf Widows' Club
Sailing Solo
Carole Singer's Christmas
Christmas Wishes
A Slippery Slope
The Perfect Christmas Plan
Be Mine
It Takes Two
Bells and Bows on Mistletoe Row

Lizzie Marshall series:
Highland Fling – book 1
Lizzie Marshall's Wedding – book 2

Goldebury Bay series:
Ninety Days of Summer – book 1
Ninety Steps to Summerhill – book 2
Ninety Days to Christmas – book 3

Hideaway Down series:
A Christmas Hideaway – book 1
Catch A Falling Star – book 2
Walking on Sunshine – book 3
Dancing in the Rain – book 4

Hall's Cross series
Deck the Halls – book 1
The Starlight Ball – book 2

Michaelmas Bay series
Christmas Secrets in Snowflake Cove – book 1
Blame it on the Moonlight – book 2

Lily Pond Lane series
The Cottage on Lily Pond Lane – four-part serial
Part One – New beginnings
Part Two – Summer secrets
Part Three – Autumn leaves
Part Four – Trick or treat
Christmas on Lily Pond Lane
Return to Lily Pond Lane
A Wedding on Lily Pond Lane
Secret Wishes and Summer Kisses on Lily Pond Lane

Wyntersleap series
Christmas at Wynter House – Book 1
New Beginnings at Wynter House – Book 2
A Wedding at Wynter House – Book 3
Love is in the Air – spin off

Merriment Bay series
Coming Home to Merriment Bay – Book 1
(four-part serial)
Part One – A Reunion
Part Two – Sparks Fly
Part Three ~ Christmas
Part Four – Starry Skies
Chasing Moonbeams in Merriment Bay – Book 2
Wedding Bells in Merriment Bay – Book 3

Seahorse Harbour series
Summer at my Sister's – book 1
Christmas at Aunt Elsie's – book 2
Just for Christmas – book 3
Tasty Treats at Seahorse Bites Café – book 4
Dreams and Schemes at The Seahorse Inn – book 5
Weddings and Reunions in Seahorse Harbour – book 6

Clementine Cove series
Christmas at Clementine Cove – book 1
Broken Hearts and Fresh Starts at Cove Café – book 2
Friendships Blossom in Clementine Cove – book 3

Norman Landing series
Saving Christmas – book 1
A not so secret Winter Wedding – book 2
Sunsets and Surprises at Seascape Café – book 3
A Date at the end of The Pier – book 4

To see a complete list of my books, or to sign up for my newsletter, go to www.emilyharvale.com/books

There's also an exclusive Facebook group for fans of my books. www.emilyharvale.com/FacebookGroup

Or scan the QR code below to see all my books on Amazon.

Printed in Great Britain
by Amazon